MW01221780

The
GREAT BRIDGE
Conspiracy

VIVISPHERE
PUBLISHING

The GREAT BRIDGE Conspiracy

TERRY QUINN

Copyright © 1979 Terry Quinn
First published in the United States by St. Martin's Press
First Published in England by Allen & Unwin
All rights reserved

ISBN 1-58776-070-3

Library of Congress Catalogue Number 2001-

www.vivisphere.com

1-800-724-1100

VIVISPHERE
PUBLISHING

Also by Terry Quinn

FICTION AND BIOGRAPHY

A Death in Brooklyn

Second Daughter: Growing Up in China, 1930-1949
(with Katherine Wei)

PLAYS AND MUSIC THEATER

A Second Chance

Rasputin

Dear Bunny, Dear Volodya

Love Hurts

Bad Evidence

Georgette's Last Rehearsal

Wilde Nights

POETRY

Mad for Newyorktown: Dark Verse and Light

To Joan and Bill Benesch

The

GREAT BRIDGE

Conspiracy

✦✦✦ Part One ✦✦✦

FEINGLASS, AWAKENED

He felt the urge to curse, though he was not a cursing man. Nothing upset Solomon Feinglass more than being roused from bed prematurely—especially now, at his age, when sleep was so hard to come by. He could tell even before the second ring that the darkness in the room was no longer seamless; that dawn had just arrived. The phone was not on the nightstand, where it should have been, but somewhere on the floor, halfway across the room. Probably Tulliver's doing. He searched about for his slippers but could not find them, and so padded barefoot in the direction of the insistent sound. It might be Kincannon again, he thought, demanding to know how much longer it was going to take him to finish the job. Or, more likely, someone from the other side calling to harass him, hoping to provoke an angry reaction. As he brushed a few strands of matted white hair from his forehead and gently uncradled the receiver, he noticed that the luminescent hands of his travel clock registered twenty-five minutes before six. That made it only four hours since he and Croft had finally abandoned their lookout posts across the street from the Plaza and gone to get some rest. "Yes? Who is it?"

"I was right, boss. Something's up. Can you get to a safe phone?"

He wanted to tell Tulliver outright that he was a fool, a bungler, a pest. "The phone is clean, Tulliver. How many times do I have to tell you that? These people don't deal in the obvious. And anyway, there could be five taps on the phone and I wouldn't budge from this bed. Now tell me what on earth you..."

"He's been sitting on a bench over here in Brooklyn for almost five hours now, hardly moving."

"Who? Who's been sitting on a bench in Brooklyn?"

"Kane, sir."

"And for this you call me at five-thirty in the morning?"

"Yes, sir. He's got loads of pens and pads with him, and it looks to me like he's getting ready to write up a storm. The way I see it, if we could get our hands on the stuff, it just might tip us off to a lot of things. Like whether this Piper guy knows what we're up to."

It pained him to admit, even to himself, that the man might be onto something. Who would have thought that Kane was the one to follow after the banquet at the restaurant? And yet he had long ago made it a rule of thumb that there was no one on either side of this business who did not deserve to be spied upon. A rule he never used to overlook. "Okay, Tulliver, you were right, I was wrong."

"Thanks, boss."

"Now don't go and spoil it, do you hear? Don't let him see you, and don't risk lifting the stuff now. We'll have plenty of time to get it, whatever it is, in San Francisco."

"Right. I won't make a move, unless..."

"No risks, Tulliver, do you hear me?"

"Right."

"Call in if anything important happens, and see to it that you make it to the plane on time tonight."

"Right. Well...good morning, sir."

"Good morning, Tulliver." He replaced the receiver on its hook, returned to bed and turned gingerly onto his left side, settling into the one position in which his humped back permitted him to sleep. "When men of the caliber of Tulliver and Kane start to control things," he mumbled to himself, "then maybe it's time to get out. Maybe it means I'm getting too old..."

Part Two

THE DIARY OF
TERENCE DANIEL KANE

Prologue

Pity me, reader. For I sit alone on this abandoned promenade and watch with heavy heart as, far across the water, the night lights of Manhattan are robbed of their brilliance by the reddish-gray fingers of dawn. I have pined all night on this promontory of Brooklyn Heights, following with my eyes the East River's black, leaden flow, but in my mind looking two hundred miles south to the Potomac and to the city of Washington, my home. Looking back to the quiet days, ten months past, before Jane and I broke up. Back to the time when I was happily employed as a mailroom clerk in the basement of the United States Capitol; when I slept in a shared bed instead of sitting up all night on a hard wooden bench, trying to compose this journal; and when my mind was not aswirl with pretensions to duplicate-bridge fame or with the Byzantine complexities of international espionage. Looking back, in short, to the days when the name "Captain Diggery Piper" was as irrelevant to my existence as the cloak-and-dagger drama in which that man has embroiled me.

As a thumbnail sketch of my background will reveal, I was used to tamer fare. My name is Terence Kane. I am thirty-one years old and a graduate of Delaware State University where I took bachelors, masters and doctorate, all in the field of comparative literature. Though I finished in the top third of my class and immediately landed a choice position at Newton Community College just outside of Boston, my career as a professor came to an untimely end when I found, after a single semester, that I was unable to turn to practical advantage all the theory I'd so carefully amassed. (A condition which, as I have more than once been told, appears to have become both general and chronic.)

Following that setback, I lowered my sights and taught English composition for the next two years at Sibley High in Dorchester, where I experienced some modest success both as teacher and career guidance counselor, but where the torpor that develops from having sold oneself short soon set in. I was haunted by the feeling that I might still be destined for greater things, for a mission in life more meaningful and more glamorous than the unsplitting of adolescents' infinitives.

My big break came three years ago, in November of 1980, when my uncle, Kevin "Spuds" O'Flaherty— then a local Democratic party chairman in the Back Bay section of Boston—won a seat in Congress and offered to take me to Washington as his speechwriter. I accepted without hesitation. Custom-made, I thought. A chance to escape the small-time world of pimples, pot parties and puppy love and take on issues of national concern. Uncle Kevin and I moved to the capital in early January. In February, he was assigned to the Post Office and Civil Service Committee. And on March 4, 1981—the very day he was scheduled to deliver his maiden speech on the floor of the House and thus to immortalize in the *Congressional Record* a masterpiece of rhetoric on which I had labored for seven weeks, he was indicted for mail fraud by a Boston grand jury. A whirlwind of feverish legal activity accounted for all his free time between indictment and conviction. But as a parting kindness to the family, I suppose, Spuds called in the few markers he'd been able to collect in his all too brief tenure as a statesman and, shortly before entering the Waltham Minimum Security Penal Facility, secured me a patronage slot in the Congressional mailroom. There I toiled gratefully, assidu-

10

ously, until one fateful night last autumn.

Yes, I was surrounded by functional illiterates. Yes, I slaved eight hours a day in the windowless depths of the Capitol for less money than I had earned at Sibley High. And yes, I had effectively retreated into the same kind of mediocre existence against which I'd earlier rebelled. But now, in a way, I was happy. Now I had learned (or at least thought I had learned) my limitations. What did it matter how I squandered my daytime hours? Once home each evening, I had Jane's company, my books, my magazines, and above all my opiate—bridge. I would play out scores of hands by myself every night, sometimes forcing Jane to take on the defense. I would read the bridge columns of the *Post* and the *Star* and of every neighborhood rag I could get my hands on. I would devour bridge newsletters, bridge bulletins, bridge journals, bridge tomes. I would lie in bed at night solving double-dummy problems and indulging in fantasies of the most wickedly revealing relay-bid sequences imaginable. Then, come Monday evening, I would swoop down like a bird of prey upon the local duplicate club, where my thirst for competing, if not for winning, would regularly be slaked.

How thin this patina of complacency must have been, for it vanished the very evening I met Piper. Just as a tourist isolated in a foreign land will latch onto the first fellow countryman he meets, so was I drawn to the Captain—my countryman in spirit if not citizenship. It was not only his articulate speech and distinctive manner of dress that attracted me, nor merely his patrician taste in food and wine, but his matchless skill at the table. How predictable it all seems now that I should have fallen under the spell of this man who, in the ten months since, has been at one time friend, at another foe; at one time bridge partner, at another opponent. A man whom, in many ways, I know no better now than I did before our acquaintance began. A superior whose orders have at times caused me qualms of conscience to obey. An adviser I have never quite grown to trust. An aggressor—to resort to Freudian terminology—with whom I find I cannot help but identify.

The sun rises less than majestically over the tenements of

Brooklyn and burns through the malodorous smog that has enshrouded this city for the entire two days we have been here. (By "we" I mean Piper, myself and the other two members of our motley Grand National Knockout team: the ever-amusing Sally McGonigle and my partner, Reginald Graves. But more of them later.) There is not one cloud in the sky, no threat of rain whatsoever; and this is good. For now that I finally feel relaxed enough to write, I do not intend to budge until this diary is completed. I begin by arranging about me the dog-eared scraps of paper upon which I've kept a running record of the Captain's more dazzling plays. And I find that, as if by magic, the details surrounding them return.

There are, of course, distractions. The people of "The City" walk by me in review. Some are early risers, some stragglers from all-night parties. Then there are others about whom I can tell nothing, for their glassy, blood-filled eyes (New York eyes, I call them) give the impression that they have never slept and perhaps never will. They all glance blankly at the notebooks stacked beside me, at the clutter of felt-tipped pens, the pyramid of deli sandwiches, the vat of lemonade—that pitiful store of supplies meant to help me through this ordeal of self-revelation. I can feel the pressure of those questioning eyes but do not so much as stare back in reply. I have no time to waste, not one minute. Fourteen hours from now I will be flying to San Francisco (I who have never ventured westward of Hershey Park, Pennsylvania), to play, and doubtless to be crushed by, one of the other seven teams still remaining in this endless Grand Nationals competition.

And yet Piper boasted last night, in his stupor, that we would not lose. That we would fight our way through the quarters and semis to the final round, there to culminate an intelligence mission which he claims has been four long years in the staging. A mission about which he has sworn me to total secrecy. (If my keeping this diary should constitute a breach of that promise, I cannot help it—the burden of absolute silence has become intolerable.) I confess to having moments of weakness, moments when I hope to God he is wrong in his grandiose calculations (although he has never once been wrong when it counted). I cannot deny that the

12

opportunity I've been given fills me with a heady rush of pride.
Yet you must believe that there are times when I would be just as
content—no, more content by far—to leap from this madcap
carousel ride to the humdrum routine of my past.

But let me tell you now how I reached this pretty pass. Let me
share with you the story of how an unassuming mail-sorter and
happy dabbler in the game of bridge was, through no fault of his
own, dragged into the vortex of a maelstrom.

Episode I

In Which the Congressional Duplicate Bridge Club Welcomes a Strange New Member into Its Fold...

(October 25, 1982)

It was seven minutes to game time in the Jefferson Lounge of the Old Senate Office Building where the Congressional Duplicate Bridge Club has met every Monday evening from 8:00 to 11:30 for the past quarter century. To form the proper impression, you must first sweep from your mind all images of the run-of-the-mill duplicate bridge gathering. The Congressional, as it is called by its frequenters, is no smoke-choked, neon-lit, noise-ridden hall littered with folding chairs, formica tabletops and a nightly crop of crumpled convention cards. No, when my distinguished co-members and I filed into the gameroom that brisk autumn evening for a pre-game cup of espresso and some shoptalk, we entered a plush environment where Persian carpets and massive tapestries soak up the genteel conversation, where parquet floors and walnut wainscoting surround one in the warmth of varnished wood, and where all forms of tobacco use, save pipe smoking, are anathema.

In short, the Congressional is an elegant, unabashedly tradition-bound congregation of legislative aides, high-powered secretaries, an occasional precocious page, and a number of the people's representatives. Senators Beatrice Winfield of Arizona

14

and Charles R. Hohine of Connecticut, and Congressmen Grabowski, Crawley and McNair of Wisconsin, Idaho and Delaware, respectively, favor us every week with their presence, while several of their colleagues stop by for an occasional game. Of course, the roster of notables was considerably longer back in the days when a pleasant game of cards was regarded by the average lawmaker as a sufficiently stimulating nighttime activity.

There are a handful of pinch-faced backbiters who, more out of envy, I am convinced, than anything else, are given to dismissing the Congressional Club as a stodgy, elitist institution. Now, it is true that the mean age of our venerable members (most of whom have long since become pillars of one community or another) is sixty-two years, and that no more than half are still spry enough to participate in anything more taxing than the annual banquet. But what the Congressional lacks in vitality, it more than makes up for in cachet.

I was searching frantically for a partner. Due to a lamentable series of failed psychic bids on my part during the previous four weeks' sessions, my girlfriend, Jane—ordinarily a model of saintly patience—had informed me that afternoon that backgammon was now the game of her choice. Nor could I blame her. Bridge was the sole blight on our otherwise ideal relationship. I don't think we ever really developed a solid partnership understanding. She, admittedly the superior player, always seemed satisfied to place third or fourth week after week with what I regarded as a maddeningly cautious brand of play. On the other hand, she appeared to resent my predilection for freshly minted bidding systems coupling a warehouseful of intricate gadgetry with an overall tone of fierce intimidation. And with what disdain she looked upon my daring leads and defensive gambits which, if I had only been able to count on the average Joe's fair share of luck, would doubtless have vaulted me long before now to the uppermost echelons of competitive bridge.

In any case, Jane had cut me off. And to make matters worse, my back-up partner, Reginald Graves (a man who does appear at times to share Jane's general estimation of my style, but who takes a considerably more philosophical attitude toward our disappoint-

15

ing results), was out of the country on business. I was on the verge of begging the assistant director himself to play with me and subjecting myself to a night of patronizing pedantry, when the club's sedate chatter was momentarily silenced by the appearance at the door of a tall, slender man of swarthily handsome demeanor. He was no younger than thirty-five, surely no older than mid-forties. But the aura of mystery which surrounded him had less to do with this ambiguity of age than it did with his strange manner of dress.

As a subscriber to *Suave Magazine*, I have developed over the years an in-depth familiarity with the world of *haute couture*, and so I was able to identify the various items of our visitor's smashing ensemble. He wore Italian leather boots—that season's Guccis, of course—over the tops of which drooped a pair of Yves Saint-Laurent knickers woven of that argyle-patterned wool that is all the rage in Paris these days. A belted, billowy tunic of, once again, European design hardly suffered for being half concealed by a knee-length worsted cape lined in satin. On the stranger's right shoulder perched a parrot, the bird's stiff, glistening plumage of chartreuse and gold working in contrast to its master's dramatic shock of black curls. The effect was, in a word, arresting.

The man strode evenly toward the partnership desk and in a clipped British accent asked Nora Graham, our perennial treasurer, for an entry. I sidled over to the desk and overheard Nora inform the gentleman that only Congress-connected personnel and their guests were allowed to compete in the game. The words of that message were stern enough, but the woman's heart was not in them. And in her eyes one could read the closest thing to naked lust that Nora had let herself feel for the past twenty years. When the man replied, it was with a smile so seductive as to aggravate her problem. Given the general state of paralysis inspired by the stranger's entrance, his resonant, liquid-toned voice seemed to fill the entire chamber.

"With all due respect, madam, I was informed at the embassy that I might be permitted to play here, and was so looking forward to the experience. I do not wish to presume, but perhaps this letter of introduction will fulfill your eligibility requirements." He

16

reached into the bone-white lining of his cape, somewhat discomfiting the parrot, which otherwise stared icily at the discombobulated Mrs. Graham. The document he displayed was printed on State Department stationery and—although I could scarcely read it from my position across the desk—appeared to bear the signature of Samuel Deatherage, our ambassador to the Court of Saint James.

"I...I see," stammered Nora. "Well, I suppose you're more than welcome to join us. But we're really not supposed to allow any...any animals in here, sir."

"Pray address me as Captain," was all he answered as he leaned forward to fill out an entry and a membership form, then signed both in a florid yet perfectly legible script: *Captain Diggery Piper.* "Now, where might I be likely to find a partner?"

No one failed to hear him. Not Constance Bartlett, who had long ago secured a partner but who now appeared willing to ditch him; not Congresswoman Crisalli, whose sheepish, bridge-hating husband might have acquiesced on the spot if the forum for the prospective switch had not been so public; and certainly not Gloria Fowler, who was closer to the Captain in age than either of the previous two contenders and was, I knew, far more likely to speak up. (The majority of the club's males, on the other hand, made silent show of resenting the way this outrageously dressed intruder was holding court.)

"What about you, my good man?" he asked me, just as Gloria was rising from her chair to announce her availability.

"Yes!" I blurted out. "That is, I was just looking for a partner myself. Of course, I'm not usually in this predicament. You see, my girlfriend and I used to play together regularly until... well, what happened was...I mean, ordinarily I would play either with her or with my friend Reginald, but he isn't...Yes, I would, sir. Captain."

"Excellent," he replied. "Excellent."

Our director, Edmund Gradys, prides himself on getting play started precisely at 8:00 P.M. , so there was little time left for proper introductions. Nor did my new acquaintance seem overly eager to elaborate on his background. In fact, all he said on the way to our table was that while he regarded ACOL as the sole civilized approach to bidding, he would deign to use "any system you fancy." I panicked as I realized that the slam-searching intricacies of traditional ACOL had become inextricably interwoven in my mind with a host of rather interesting improvements recently elucidated by the promising young London-based star, Rutherford Hastings-Bromley, in the lead article of *Bridge in Britain*, Volume 54, Number 2. I decided to play it safe and beat a hasty retreat to good old Standard American.

Piper took the South seat and proceeded to nod in every direction to the club membership which, to a player, was still staring dumbly at the eccentric figure he cut. How strange it is to think back on that moment now; to read again in those onlooking faces the subtle mixture of interest, amusement and, I will say it, condescension. This dandy's presence would be suffered, they were thinking to themselves, for a week, at most two, by which time the Congressional's lofty standards of play would have resulted in his quiet withdrawal. How heartily my co-members would have laughed at me then if I had predicted that our cozy, low-keyed club was about to be transformed into a showcase for the Captain's brilliance. And, even more preposterous, that my own mercurial ascent into the rarefied ether of national bridge stardom was to begin that selfsame night.

Once we were permitted to begin play, Piper pulled his cards from board one, then receded into a trance of concentration from which he would not emerge during the remainder of that fascinating evening except as a result of direct provocation. I present now the very first hand we played and stress that it was not chosen over the twenty-three that followed it for any particular reason, so consistently inspired was my partner's technique:

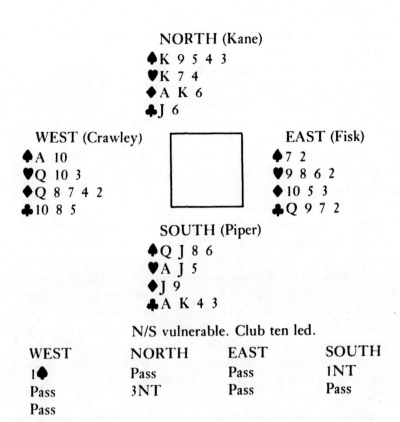

NORTH (Kane)
♠ K 9 5 4 3
♥ K 7 4
♦ A K 6
♣ J 6

WEST (Crawley)
♠ A 10
♥ Q 10 3
♦ Q 8 7 4 2
♣ 10 8 5

EAST (Fisk)
♠ 7 2
♥ 9 8 6 2
♦ 10 5 3
♣ Q 9 7 2

SOUTH (Piper)
♠ Q J 8 6
♥ A J 5
♦ J 9
♣ A K 4 3

N/S vulnerable. Club ten led.

WEST	NORTH	EAST	SOUTH
1♦	Pass	Pass	1NT
Pass	3NT	Pass	Pass
Pass			

Sitting West at that first table (I can recall his haughty expression as clearly as if he were sitting next to me now on this bench) was Congressman Obadiah Crawley, fourteen-term Idaho Democrat, Chairman of the House Ethics Committee and, in his role as self-proclaimed expert on parliamentary procedure, the scourge of every freshman representative who dared to hold forth on the floor of the House. Speaker Wright's official parliamentarian might just as well have resigned the day he was hired, for Crawley was far more conversant than he not only with *Robert's Rules of Order* as revised by Thomas Jefferson but with every tortuous citation in the volumes of *Deschler's Precedents*, and had no qualms about calling the poor man's attention to each and every digression from what was proper. Needless to say, he conducted himself with the same authoritarian air when riding herd on the members of the Ethics Committee.

Now, if the Congressman had applied to himself those standards of propriety he required his peers to uphold, he might have inspired less fear and more respect. But alas, as the members of the House and of the Congressional Bridge Club alike had found out over the years, Obadiah Crawley had a considerably healthier regard for the letter of the law—any law—than he did for its spirit. At the bridge table, for example, he was the sort of player who takes maximum advantage of his hulking stature, his booming voice, his indisputable aura of importance, often cowing more talented players with a curmudgeon's stare and managing to equalize the odds through the exercise of what he liked to call "gamesmanship." In reality, he has long been suspected of transmitting and receiving improper information through ploys so discreet, so deniable, that no opponent would ever take the draconian measure of publicly charging him with cheating.

Sitting opposite Crawley that evening was Mortimer Fisk, the Congressman's weasel-eyed administrative assistant and unquestioning accomplice in all things shady. What the boss wanted done, Mortimer did. They were the image of Greenstreet and Lorre.

I watched Captain Piper wait patiently for Crawley to begin the bidding and regretted that I had not had time to warn him against this pair's shenanigans. The glaringly inappropriate delay, I knew from past experience, meant one of four things: (a) the Congressman was barely short of sufficient point count to open; (b) he was about to make a psychic bid in a suit he did not hold; (c) both of the above; or (d) he held cards that would justify a straightforward opening but wished to promote the false impression that (a), (b) or (c) obtained.

"A spade," barked Obadiah as he frowned one last time at his punchless holding and, for one reason or another, cocked a furry white eyebrow.

His delay and eventual bid had left me in a quandary. I decided for the time being to take his call at face value and so passed. Fisk too passed and Piper bid a notrump. Now when the bidding came

20

back to me I knew that Crawley had probably psyched. But since he and Fisk made no bones about opening four-card majors (although their convention card indicated otherwise), I could still not tell for certain that Piper held anything better than a flimsy stopper in spades and that Crawley would not show up with a stack of them against us. I opted for a three notrump call which was quickly passed out.

"Excuse me a moment, gentlemen," said Crawley. Before I had time to react he was passing behind me, ostensibly on his way toward the coffee urn. And you may be sure he passed behind the Captain on his way back. Again I had let my partner down. I had failed to warn him that when playing against "the Chairman," as the denizens of the Hill were wont to call Obadiah Crawley, club members customarily held their cards closer to the chest than when competing against a less vigilant opponent. Lest you brand my suspicions as paranoid, I would point out that upon reseating himself, Crawley avoided the natural lead of the diamond four which would have given up a trick, passed over the heart three which would have had the same result, and hit upon the safe ten of clubs.

The dummy came down and Piper got the news that we had been steered into an inferior contract. "Surprised, Cap'n?" asked Obadiah with a meaningful chuckle. One which Mortimer Fisk was quick to echo.

"Not really," Piper replied. "I find that situations like these tend to bring out the best in one's game, don't you?"

"Can't say for sure," countered the Congressman as if he did not have a complete picture of the deal. "But offhand, I imagine the situation I'd want to be in, if I were you, that is, would be four spades." Though reprehensible in the extreme, this gloating was certainly based on a solid foundation of fact. Eleven tricks are there for the taking in the suit contract, even if the heart finesse loses, while notrump figures to make four when spades makes five and five when spades makes six. We'd been fixed but good.

But if the Captain was discouraged by these developments, he showed no sign of it. He covered the ten of clubs with dummy's Jack and, when Fisk produced the Queen and Crawley chuckled

21

again, calmly played his Ace. Now he led the Queen of spades. The Congressman took his Ace and tabled the eight of clubs, which Piper allowed to win the trick. Crawley's eyes bulged with confusion and delight, and I must confess that my own reaction was to wonder if I had not acted too rashly in taking this new-comer under my wing.

"I guess you limeys play cards a little different than we do," crowed the Chairman. "Over here we tend not to let eights win when we're holding Kings."

"But Congressman," Piper protested, "how on earth could you know that I, and not your partner, hold the club King?" This appeared to fluster Crawley for an instant, but he recovered soon enough.

"Why because... because of your notrump overcall, naturally. Your convention card indicates that that bid shows fifteen to eighteen points, doesn't it? So you've got to have that King to reach even the minimum of your bid."

"I see, I see," said Piper who, I realize now, must have deduced instantaneously that Crawley's statement marked him with the heart and diamond Queens. For only the player who could add those two honor cards to East's Queen at trick one, West's Ace at trick two, and the thirteen points in dummy would know that South had to have been dealt the club King to fill out his promised count. At the time, I thought the Congressman had successfully eluded the Captain's grasp. But I see now that, even at that early stage, the man was being fitted for a noose.

Obadiah Crawley gratefully accepted the unlooked-for gift of a club trick and fired back the five of that suit. This Piper captured with his King, sluffing a heart in the North hand. Needing all the remaining tricks in order to post a good score, Diggery now began running his spade winners, and the tenor of the hand gradually changed. The first three spades seemed to present our opponents with no problems since East could play a spade and two hearts, maintaining his diamond and club guards, while West played a spade and two diamonds, thus preserving his stoppers in diamonds and hearts. But when the final spade came down in this position:

22

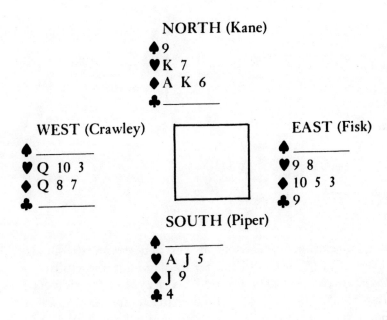

NORTH (Kane)
♠ 9
♥ K 7
♦ A K 6
♣ ———

WEST (Crawley)
♠ ———
♥ Q 10 3
♦ Q 8 7
♣ ———

EAST (Fisk)
♠ ———
♥ 9 8
♦ 10 5 3
♣ 9

SOUTH (Piper)
♠ ———
♥ A J 5
♦ J 9
♣ 4

the Chairman felt the tightening of the knot. Once Fisk blithely dumped another heart and Piper discarded his diamond nine, Crawley was forced to surrender his half of the diamond defense in order to protect the heart Queen.

"My guess is that makes one down, one to go," pronounced Diggery with equanimity. Next he cashed dummy's King of hearts and then called for the seven:

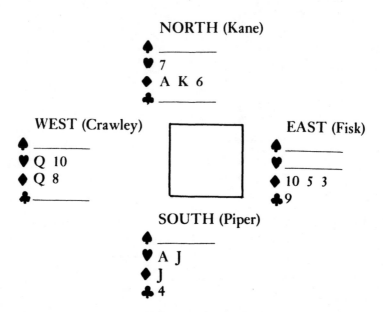

NORTH (Kane)
♠ _____
♥ 7
♦ A K 6
♣ _____

WEST (Crawley)
♠ _____
♥ Q 10
♦ Q 8
♣ _____

EAST (Fisk)
♠ _____
♥ _____
♦ 10 5 3
♣ 9

SOUTH (Piper)
♠ _____
♥ A J
♦ J
♣ 4

What the nine of spades had done to West in hearts and diamonds, the seven of hearts now did to East in diamonds and clubs.

This way and that shot the tiny black eyes of the desperate Mortimer Fisk as he scoured his holding in vain for some means of escape. With a pitiful, pleading glance toward his employer he finally dropped a diamond to the table, whereupon Obadiah Crawley threw down his cards in disgust. His hoary eyebrows contracted; his jaw seemed to harden; his lips formed into a spiteful, mocking curl. "I hope you realize you've just handed them an extra overtrick," he brayed.

"Yessir. I...I'm awfully sorry, sir."

"...And that by making five notrump they'll score 660 to everyone else's 650..."

"Yessir. I must have failed to keep a correct count of the diamonds, sir."

Bull! I would have cried out in that mealy-mouthed Fisk's defense if I'd had any idea at the time of the Hobson's choice the Captain had presented him. But it was Diggery himself who took the man's part.

24

"What would you have had Mr. Fisk discard at trick ten?" he asked Crawley. "The club nine?" (I must admit I was in awe of Diggery Piper at that moment, as I suppose I have been ever since. There is a quality of indomitability about him; an effulgence of what you would have to call character. I saw it that very first night when he stood up to Crawley's bullying as none of us before had dared to do, and since then I've seen it time and time again. With all his faults of British stiffness, a more than occasional lapse into sarcasm and, of course, his almost insufferable vanity, the man nevertheless has spine.)

A fuming Crawley studied Fisk's last four cards, hesitated a moment, then blustered: "I'm not talking about now. He...he should have overtaken my club eight at trick three when you rectified the count by ducking. Then he could have led hearts safely and...and broken the squeeze." His usually stentorian bass was now undermined by indecision. It was clear that he was grasping at straws.

"Not so," observed Piper, who seemed more composed than ever. "There would still have been sufficient means of communication available for executing the double squeeze. And even if the distribution had been such that the overtake and shift would have succeeded, I certainly think it would be unfair to expect one's partner to find such a play. You must remember that very few of us, Congressman, have developed the fine art of defending as if all four hands were in view."

In an apparent show of agreement with this analysis, the parrot squawked. And the Chairman skulked off in defeat.

Episode II

In Which It Is Explained How the Diamond Eight Kept Captain Diggery Piper in the New World...

(November 1, 1982)

It was ten minutes before midnight and I was beside myself with exhilaration. For a good quarter hour I had stalked up and down the southeast stretch of Pennsylvania Avenue like a man possessed, trying to recall the name of the bar where Diggery had said I might join him, searching in vain among the ebb and flow of revelers constantly entering and exiting from the cluster of night-spots that lie between Second and Fourth Streets. Oh, how sorely I was tempted to buttonhole some pert senatorial caseworker, say, sit her down on a barstool and inform her that for the first time in my bridge career, I had taken first-place honors two weeks in a row. How I would have loved to regale her with a point-by-point description of the evening's many highlights. Sure, I would have recounted the details of Diggery's incredible eleven-card crossruff on board six, and his clairvoyant safety play on board eleven, and perhaps even his daring Deschapelles Coup on the very last deal of the night. But I would have taken care, too, to stress the subtler and, I would maintain, more telling motifs, such as my own martyrlike display of forbearance and sacrifice in permitting my partner to become declarer on nineteen of the twenty-four hands

26

we played. But no, she would have to wait. After all, it was Piper himself who deserved to hear the good news first.

"Diggery!" I shouted, having recognized his distinctive silhouette from almost a block away. He was striding into the Hawk and Dove at Third and Pennsylvania, apparently out of earshot. I hustled down the cold, windswept avenue, simply bursting with anticipation.

I found the Captain ensconced in a toasty alcove of the pub's rearmost room where three female attendants were seeing to his every need—one delivering a pony of Pernod, one setting before him a half dozen succulent Chincoteague selects, a third draping his cape over an empty chair and slipping what appeared to be a hatcheck into the breast pocket of his tunic. He looked pleased indeed with the thoroughness of their ministrations, but something (I could not for the life of me tell what) seemed to be missing.

"Terence, how nice. Do sit down and join me. Sorry to abandon you at the scorer's table like that, old boy, but I always find all that factoring and whatnot to be far and away the dullest part of the evening. I waited for you at Duddington's, you know, but when you didn't show by a quarter to twelve, I thought I'd see what else the Avenue had to offer."

"We won again!" I cried, no longer able to contain my joy. "Just as you predicted. And by fifteen matchpoints!"

"Oh? I should have guessed nineteen or twenty," he replied with a wry British arching of the eyebrows. "I say, would you like to try one of these? They're top drawer, really." He was holding out an oyster. When I refused, he tilted his head back, raised the shell slightly above his mouth and let the viscous meat slither onto the back of his tongue. There it was savored for an instant or two before being dispatched with a slow-motion swallow. "Only a Philistine would chew such an exquisite creature," he observed.

To someone as obsessed with bridge as I was, as vulnerable to the spells of elation and depression that that game so often casts upon its bleary-eyed victims, this show of supreme indifference to our results was a mystery; and coming from someone as talented as the Captain, almost an affront. To think I would have sold my soul at that moment to be able to play half as well as he could,

27

while all he would talk about was shellfish. Perhaps more than anything else, it is this difference in attitude toward the game that has been responsible for the distance that has always remained between us. A distance I was foolish enough to think I could make disappear that night.

"You can't imagine how I feel," I persisted. "This has never happened to me before. I mean, I won once in March of '69 and once, pending an as yet unadjudicated appeal, in July of '81, but never on two consecutive Mondays!"

"Calm yourself, ducks, no use getting exercised. Who knows? Perhaps even greater triumphs await. Here, why don't you let me spring for a pint or two in celebration?"

For the better part of an hour we sat there talking over the evening's hands, planning our next week's strategy and doggedly polishing off mug after mug of Watney's and stout. It occurred to me then that I knew next to nothing about this man. Not what he did for a living, where he'd come from, why he wore the clothes he did. Nothing. Piqued with curiosity, I decided at last to steer the conversation away from that night's bridge and toward more personal matters. "So what exactly are you doing here, anyway?" I began.

"I beg your pardon?"

"You know, what's your business here in Washington?" My shift in the mailroom was due to start at 7:30 A.M. so I was not inclined to beat around the bush.

"I . . . I have no business here, actually. Nor anywhere else for the time being. You might say I'm on extended tour. Yes, a very leisurely tour of your lovely East Coast."

"I see. A vacation?"

"Nothing that formal, really."

"Oh? Then just how did you end up here in the States?"

He hesitated, took a sip of the Pernod that he nursed on the side the whole time we were there, then answered. "The reason, as much as any other, was the diamond eight."

"The diamond eight?"

"Precisely. But allow me to elaborate. I am a Londoner by birth, a seaman by training and profession, and a life-long fancier

28

of tallmasted sailing ships by avocation. Six years ago this past spring I applied for what I thought at the time would be a temporary leave from my position as Director of the British Academy of Sail Training in Liverpool in order to participate in your Bicentennial celebration. I was the guest of a fellow countryman, one Sir Geoffrey Trumbull, Captain of the brigantine *Cressida*. That magnificent square-rigged relic of the clipper days was slated to take part in a project called Operation Sail..."

"I remember. The regatta of thirty or forty nineteenth-century ships that sailed into New York Harbor on July 4, 1976."

"The very same."

"Is that when you first started dressing like that? I mean... Excuse me, I..."

"It's quite all right, old boy. Actually I'd developed a taste for dramatic attire well before then—a taste which in no way conflicted, I might point out, with the delightfully antiquarian bent of the Academy."

"I see."

"Well, our trans-Atlantic journey was uneventful enough, but when the *Cressida* embarked on her voyage back to fair England, she was minus one Piper." Here the Captain quaffed the last of his liqueur, obviously relishing both its licorice bouquet and the rhetorical effect of his pause. "You will want the particulars. On the eve of what you Yanks insist on referring to as your Day of Independence, we were anchored in the halcyon waters of Sandy Hook, just off the northern New Jersey shore. There Trumbull and I were being properly fleeced by two of the *Cressida*'s sleazier mates in a cutthroat session of bridge..."

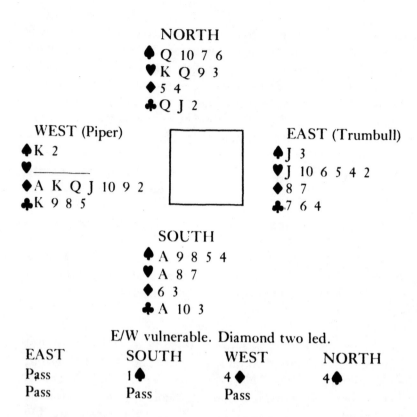

NORTH
♠ Q 10 7 6
♥ K Q 9 3
♦ 5 4
♣ Q J 2

WEST (Piper)
♠ K 2
♥ ———
♦ A K Q J 10 9 2
♣ K 9 8 5

EAST (Trumbull)
♠ J 3
♥ J 10 6 5 4 2
♦ 8 7
♣ 7 6 4

SOUTH
♠ A 9 8 5 4
♥ A 8 7
♦ 6 3
♣ A 10 3

E/W vulnerable. Diamond two led.

EAST	SOUTH	WEST	NORTH
Pass	1♠	4♦	4♠
Pass	Pass	Pass	

"...Now Sir Geoffrey," Piper continued, as he scribbled the hand you see above on a Hawk and Dove napkin and flipped it before me, "enjoys a reputation in the admiralty as an avid bridger. What is less widely appreciated, however, is the fact that his intellect, cunning and powers of concentration are far better suited to the game popularly known as 'Go Fish.' Well, when as West I produce the underlead of the decade, declarer covers my deuce with dummy's four and drops his trey under the befuddled Sir Geoffrey's seven. One glance at North's hand and I realize that I am involved in a classic deal and that I have acquitted myself of every responsibility. I have guarded against finding a singleton diamond in either the North or South hand by refusing to postpone my underlead until the second trick in favor of an exploratory King, and I have maneuvered us into position for the heart ruff that will cause declarer to go set. For as you can see, a two-step endplay awaits the myopic West defender who plays out his Ace and King of diamonds at tricks one and two."

"Sure," I said with the conviction of someone who would never have been so myopic as to cash his two winners right off the bat. I then took a lucky stab in the dark. "Sooner or later you'd have to give up a trick in clubs or spades."

"Just so. But now our heart ruff would take the place of the natural spade trick and the trump King would serve instead as a safe exit card. We would end up with two diamonds, a ruff and a club. Well, I heave a mental sigh of relief at the success of my gamble and sit back to await the obligatory heart shift. 'Queer goings-on,' says Trumbull with an exasperating chortle, 'but if the bloke can't top the seven, he'll have an even tougher time of it with the eight, wot!' And he plunks that bloody card on the table. I win the trick perforce but I do not entirely despair..." (Here the Captain began perspiring at being faced once again—if only in memory—with the enormity of Trumbull's transgression.) "...No, if that cretinous captain holds the trump Jack once protected, I calmly reason, we're still home safe. For when I continue with yet a third diamond, conceding a ruff and sluff, any play in dummy but the spade Queen will net us an uppercut when my partner's Knave forces declarer's trump Ace. I can then take my King at the first opportunity and get out unscathed with the spade deuce, knowing that I must still come to a club trick. And even if South rises with the spade Queen on my diamond continuation, pitches a club in hand, then plays Ace-low of trumps with the thought of coercing me into giving him a free club finesse, I'll save the day by slyly dumping my trump King under his Ace and promoting Trumbull's hoped-for Jack."

"Brilliant!" I gushed. "That's just brilliant!"

"Yes," Piper agreed, "and flawless, save for the fact that it assumes so much as a thimbleful of common sense at the opposite end of the table. Well, I lay down my diamond Ace and declarer throws a club from dummy. 'Think!' I want to shout to my partner. 'Think, think, think! Even if you can't work it out that this is a purposeful concession of a ruff and sluff, even if you don't

31

see the dire prospect of my being endplayed, even if adding all your hearts to all the hearts in dummy gives you no clue as to my void, at least ask yourself why I ran the risk of trying to reach your hand at trick one by underleading the Ace that now stares you in the face.' But Sir Geoffrey hesitates a moment, then gaily tosses off a heart and boasts, 'Not likely to find this old sea dog trumping his partner's Aces!' Well, South, who has experienced no difficulty whatsoever in deciphering my crystalline signals, now ruffs and hastens to cash the spade Ace and to lead out the trump five in this unfortunate position:

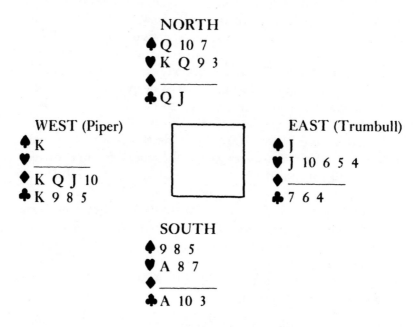

NORTH
♠ Q 10 7
♥ K Q 9 3
♦ ——————
♣ Q J

WEST (Piper)
♠ K
♥ ——————
♦ K Q J 10
♣ K 9 8 5

EAST (Trumbull)
♠ J
♥ J 10 6 5 4
♦ ——————
♣ 7 6 4

SOUTH
♠ 9 8 5
♥ A 8 7
♦ ——————
♣ A 10 3

thereby confronting me with the same suicidal choice I have been striving to avoid from the outset. This time there was no escaping. This time Trumbull had endplayed me for good."

"That's terrible," I commiserated. "Such a waste." It was past closing time now and the manager of the bar was using the establishment's light switches to convey that message. I was determined, however, to hear the end of Piper's tale. "So what did you do?"

"Vacated the premises, of course."

"You certainly do stand on principle."

"Principle, balderdash! We were playing for tuppence a point. One more fiasco like that and I would have owed those bos'ns my boots. No, I demanded then and there to be shuttled by dory to the dark Jersey shore and proceeded to put as much terrain as possible between myself and the *Cressida*."

"And you never went back?"

"What I've seen of your country—Salem, Boston, New York and now Washington—I've enjoyed immensely. I will return to England but in my own good time. All in my own good time."

When we finally rose to leave, the bar was completely empty. The floor had been swept and mopped and the chairs stacked upside down on their tables. Diggery paid the bill and left an extravagant tip with our waitress, who insisted on helping him with his cape. We then made our way to the front door, where Piper presented his check to the attendant.

"I didn't know a hat was part of that outfit of yours," I said.

"It isn't," he replied as he dropped two dollars into the silver tray, relieved the woman of his parrot, and exited into the chill morning air.

Episode III

In Which the Captain Is Smitten...
(November 8, 1982)

And the pitiful thing is, I believed him. I actually believed that Diggery was a Bicentennial leftover, a self-sufficient loner whose fate it was to drift up and down the Atlantic shoreline like some buoyant hunk of flotsam. I distinctly recall what Jane, my Cassandra, had to say when I repeated the Captain's story to her. The single word "Baloney" was the extent of her response. But I discounted her opinion at the time since I thought it was probably tainted by the anger she felt at having been wakened from a dead sleep and made to listen to a detailed account of Diggery Piper's genius.

All the same, I should have asked Piper how he supported himself financially, how he rated such preferential treatment by our State Department, how...But what difference would it have made? I know now what line of work he's in and who pays him. I know too that he would never have told me back then. No, I was to be kept totally in the dark in those days, as were all of the members of the Congressional Club. All but two, that is.

I am running far ahead of my narrative. Suffice it to say that I was blinded by our laserlike streak to success. For years I had

34

spent my Monday nights scraping and clawing and earning my master points in increments of tenths and fifths. And now I am suddenly handed three quarters of a point and first-place honors two weeks running. What did I care about how I had come into my windfall? What did I care how Piper had insinuated himself into the club? How could I have suspected back then that I was being used?

Oh, but reader, I had indeed been used and, having already served my function, was due to be flicked away like the filter of a smoked cigarette. It happened the third time we were supposed to play together— November 8th of last year. As I think back on that night, the pangs of rejection and the sting of gullibility return. For it was then that Diggery showed no compunction whatsoever about... No, let me put you in my place. Let me present you with no more evidence than the insensitive, I would even say boorish, behavior of which I was the victim that evening and let us see if you would have solved on the spot a conundrum that had me stumped for the better part of a month.

"Oooooooh, what a cute little birdie! Where'd you get her?" A slender white hand reached up and chucked the Captain's parrot beneath the beak, visibly upsetting the bird no end.

So Sally McGonigle was back from her trip abroad. As the fairest member of the secretarial pool maintained by the Senate Foreign Relations Committee, she was said to have Chairman Galetta wrapped tightly around her marvelously tapered pinkie. No mean feat, that, for an Oklahoma maiden of twenty-four years, notwithstanding the fact that the Senator is well known for the special pride he takes in personally shepherding inexperienced female staffers through the vagaries of national policymaking. In matters of salary, personal leave and "work"-related travel, Sally is the envy of all her peers. And in the matter of physical beauty, the Hill-wide consensus among male lawmakers and their aides is that she has no equal. Yet even Sally herself must realize that in the matter of native intelligence, there are precious few individuals indeed who would be eager to trade places with her.

35

At the time, of course, Piper was not aware of the fact that Miss McGonigle's personal deck, to paraphrase an apt cliché, contained considerably fewer than fifty-two cards, and he simply gazed upon her in an attitude of wonder. I was anxious to purchase an entry, hurry to our table, and discuss the advisability of adding to our growing arsenal of defensive hardware a recently published panoply of Journalist lead refinements, but I could see that the Captain's mind was elsewhere. Slowly, I am tempted to say lasciviously, his eyes swept over Sally's dazzling auburn tresses and ermine-white complexion, her dimpled chin, and her slightly parted lips, which revealed an infinitesimal yet infuriatingly seductive fissure between her two front teeth. And that was not the extent of it. I will admit that Diggery could not be said to have abandoned himself to an outright head-to-toe ogle, but neither were the sensual contours of Sally's willowy figure entirely escaping his notice. It would not take him long to learn, however, that the perfection of those bodily attributes ran in absolute inverse proportion to the poor woman's grasp of all things relating to bridge.

I was halfway through cramming the negative-double box on my convention card with the laundry list of dire warnings my pet variations require when my duty became clear. Piper, I thought, had probably not even heard Sally's question, so deep was he sunk in his reverie. "Miss Sally McGonigle," I began (vaguely recalling some precept of salutatory etiquette which, in opposite-gender situations, proscribes the mentioning of the female before the male, save when the latter is a man of the cloth, a head of state, or a duly commissioned sea captain), "I'd like to introduce Captain Diggery Piper." I should probably have warned him then and there with a wink, a roll of the eyes or some other signal that, from the point of view of expertise, Sally was not one of the club's stronger players; that, indeed, if our bylaws regarding eligibility had not included Congressional committee staff members within their scope, she might well have been home playing solitaire that night.

They gazed at each other, visibly pleased, before the word

36

"Java..." finally escaped from Diggery's lips.

"*Yo, tambièn*," replied Sally with a nervous smile. "*Encontada*, I'm sure." Knowing her as I did, I was sure that her worry had less to do with deciphering exactly what had been said to her than it did with revealing the decidedly un-Castilian lilt of her own Texarkana Spanish, which, she quickly apologized, was "pretty darn rusty." This should have been Piper's first clue.

"No, no," he explained, emerging from his trance. "I was answering your question about my parrot. Her name is Hermione and she comes from the island of Java."

Sally looked even more lost than usual, so I again interrupted. "Miss McGonigle is one of our regular members, Captain, but she's been away for about a month now on a junk... er, study mission aimed at—let's see, you told me once, Sally, but I may not have gotten it straight—measuring the benefits and countervailing drawbacks of bringing Kuwait on board as a NATO ally."

"Bahrein," she corrected, pronouncing that emirate's name as no one else ever has or ever will.

"Oh, yes, Bahrein. I suppose the thinking is that the size of that country's oil supply compensates nicely for the fact that it happens to be located more than three thousand miles from the North Atlantic?" Admittedly this delay had made me a bit testy.

"Please, Terence," Piper chided, "let's not badger the lady with dreary shoptalk. In any event, I'm sure Miss McGonigle is hardly at liberty to share with us the particulars surrounding her... her fascinating mission."

I apologized and began manufacturing some harmless chatter when I noticed that the two of them would have been satisfied simply to stare at one another all night long. "How's Reginald?" I finally asked.

"Who?"

"Why, I believe Terence is referring to Reginald Graves, Miss McGonigle, a research assistant on the staff of the House Foreign Affairs Committee and one of your colleagues, I am told, on the study mission of which you speak." I did not specifically recall having told the Captain about Reginald's participation in that project, but assumed at the time that the information must have made its way into our rambling conversation at the Hawk and Dove.

"Oh, *that* Reginald. He's fine. Just dandy."

"I must compliment you, Miss McGonigle, on your gown. It's most fetching."

"Well, thank you, Captain. Only, I wish you'd call me Sally."

"Allow me to suggest a compromise. I will call you Miss Sally, if you have no objection."

"None at all, Captain, none at all."

I had listened to quite enough of this saccharine exchange and was about to pull Piper bodily to our table when I heard him ask Sally if she had a partner for the evening. "But Diggery!" I protested.

"Darn it, no," she complained in her dust-dry prairie drawl. "And don't you know, there's not a soul left over at the partner-ship desk but that crotchety ol' Penelope Gumpers. I'll tell you, last time I played with that woman we must've said all of about two words to each other. And we pulled in dead last on top of it."

"Well, I'd be honored to be your partner, Miss Sally."

"What?" I was beside myself with rage.

"You would? My, that's neighborly of you. But I've got to warn you, some people've told me I don't play this game too well. I mean, fair's fair. I'd sure hate to spoil your night."

"Miss Sally," Piper assured her as they walked arm in arm toward what by rights should have been my table, "I find it difficult to imagine how you could possibly spoil any man's night."

"Gonna let you know right off the bat, Kane. Don't want to hear any of your nonsense bids. Got that?" The down-to-business voice of Penelope Gumpers.

"Straight Goren," I promised her as we sat down at table six with, of all people, Piper and McGonigle. It turned out to be my table after all.

"And don't try any fancy-pants leads or, what's it you call

38

them, those 'fruit-preference signals,' either." How that woman loved to feign ignorance.

"No, ma'am, I promise."

Now, Penelope Gumpers is one of those well-born, reasonably intelligent individuals whose defense against the fact that their wits do not quite match their wealth is a lifelong debunking campaign. You must know the type. A folksy brand of hostility is made to substitute for the civil manners and correct grammar of which they are perfectly capable, and cynicism is palmed off as insight. As long as I've known her, Penelope has waged a holy war against people she refers to as "pseudo-intellectuals." (When she pronounces that damning word she puckers her flaccid lips and draws out the first syllable until it captures the timbre, if not the volume and pitch, of a prize-winning hog call.) And by her insufferably provincial lights, the term seems to encompass all of *homo sapiens*, with the exception of her family and forebears.

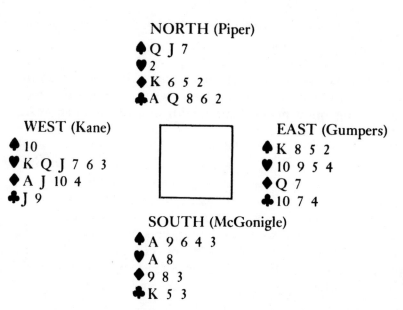

NORTH (Piper)
♠ Q J 7
♥ 2
♦ K 6 5 2
♣ A Q 8 6 2

WEST (Kane)
♠ 10
♥ K Q J 7 6 3
♦ A J 10 4
♣ J 9

EAST (Gumpers)
♠ K 8 5 2
♥ 10 9 5 4
♦ Q 7
♣ 10 7 4

SOUTH (McGonigle)
♠ A 9 6 4 3
♥ A 8
♦ 9 8 3
♣ K 5 3

Both sides vulnerable. Heart King led.

NORTH	EAST	SOUTH	WEST
1♣	Pass	1♠	Dbl.
1NT	Pass	2♠	Pass
3NT	Pass	4♣	Pass
4♥	Pass	5♣	Pass
5♥	Pass	Pass (!)	Dbl.
6♠	Pass	Pass	Dbl.
Pass	Pass	Pass	

Sally McGonigle had scampered to the South seat before we began playing the hand you see here ("I just get so confused by those silly ol' scoresheets!"). She now said to Piper, "Oh, by the way, the only conventions I play are Blackwood for Aces and, whatchamacallit, that club thing over notrump." She then scooped up her hand so quickly that Diggery was unable to ascertain just what she meant by "that club thing over notrump." The ethics of the situation clearly dictated that he wait until the completion of the first hand before attempting to resolve the ambiguity. Piper confessed to me later that he assumed she had meant Gerber and not Stayman, and that in any case it probably would not matter. As things turned out, she meant Stayman and not Gerber. And it definitely did matter.

The Captain opened a club and Sally, relieved that her responsibility seemed so straightforward, responded one spade. Diggery bid a notrump over my takeout double and Sally followed with a sheepish two spades. Now Piper executed a patently sexist leap to three notrump—a gambling mastermind of a call unabashedly designed to keep his partner out of the declarer's seat. This bid, however, left Sally helpless with doubt. Her eyes narrowed ominously and her nose fell victim to a fit of lapine twitches. In the end, the lack of a diamond stopper scared her into a four-club bid, which she meant as showing support for her partner's original suit but which Diggery took, following a silent appeal to that one authority to whom even he deferred, as the initiation of "the club thing." He dutifully bid four hearts to show his one ace, and in response to Sally's frantic five clubs, revealed his sole King with a five heart call.

"All right, already!" Sally sighed with a resigned hunch of the shoulders, and passed. That is correct. She passed.

I would have bartered my birthright for the chance to fathom the depths of Piper's despair when he realized that with some fifteen to seventeen spades and clubs between them, he and Sally had settled in what figured to be a three- or four-card heart fit. It is true that in light of what subsequently transpired, such a reading would amount to scant consolation. But a lesson I have learned about bridge in particular and about life in general is that the choice between scant consolation and no consolation is a simple one.

And now, dear reader, a confession. This deal and many others similar to it both before and since have forced me to confront in myself a rather unsettling character defect. By name, naked greed. It would seem that my ego is not constituted in such a way as to allow a five-heart bid to go by unrepudiated when I am staring at approximately half a dozen tricks. "Double," I pronounced in a dulcet tone of voice. And in truth I did not care

41

whether or whither they fled, for I was convinced that they were already way above their heads. Consider this: they could hardly have the points for a club slam; Penelope had to be sitting on a spade stack; and my ten cards and eleven points in the red suits would subject any diamond, heart or notrump contract to a terminal case of mayhem.

Oblivious to such harsh realities, Piper vaulted to six spades, an action which I felt called for, and which indeed received, a resounding double from your humble diarist. I led my King of hearts and sat back with vulturelike patience as the Captain's dummy appeared.

Envision, if you can, the cast of Sally's face as she stared at her paltry twenty-three-point holding, and as the missing King of trumps and diamond honors ricocheted like so many bats in the murky caverns of her mind. "Where're your hearts?" she almost screamed. "That's your heart suit, that deuce?"

"Now, now, Miss Sally," the Captain consoled her, "I'm certain we'll iron out these minor differences in bidding style as the evening progresses. You just settle down and do your best with what's before you." I have no doubt but that he had long since written the hand off as an unmitigated disaster. Nor would it surprise me to learn that he felt then some measure of remorse over having cast me aside prematurely.

"Well, it looks pretty bad, but I'll give it my darnedest." Sally began by winning with her Ace and ruffing the eight of hearts in dummy. She then called for the trump Queen at trick three. Judging from the quaking of her voice, I assumed she was aware of the fact that a losing finesse in trumps, coupled with an offside diamond Ace, would spell about minus 800. But when the Queen held she pushed the Jack, and her face gradually brightened. Until I showed out.

"Dang!" she cried. "I thought sure I had that King good as corralled." Sally did then what she always does when she encounters an unfortunate trump break, that is, scramble to rake in as many sidesuit winners as she can get her lovely hands on. She played to her King of clubs and led low toward dummy in diamonds. I rose with my Ace, then paused to ponder all the

42

possibilities. Particularly threatening, it seemed, was the chance that Sally had started out with three hearts and a singleton diamond. I should point out here that if Penelope Gumpers had subscribed to the avant-garde concept of giving count, she would have discarded up-down on the first two heart tricks and my problem would have been solved. But with no such signal to guide me, I was left to guess whether or not South still held a heart. When I finally chose what seemed to me to be the safest continuation (that of the heart Queen) in the position you see below, Penelope fell prey to an involuntary shudder.

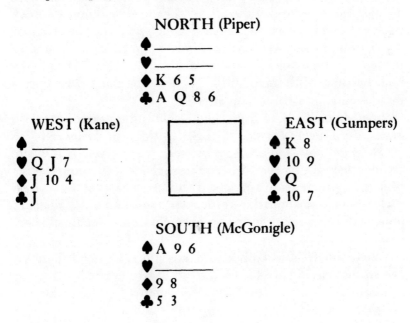

NORTH (Piper)
♠ _____
♥ _____
♦ K 6 5
♣ A Q 8 6

WEST (Kane)
♠ _____
♥ Q J 7
♦ J 10 4
♣ J

EAST (Gumpers)
♠ K 8
♥ 10 9
♦ Q
♣ 10 7

SOUTH (McGonigle)
♠ A 9 6
♥ _____
♦ 9 8
♣ 5 3

"You, too, see what is about to happen, do you not, madam?" Diggery whispered to my partner.

"Quiet!" Sally ordered. "It's bad enough you got me into this mess with your weirdo heart bids. At least don't make things any worse."

"I beg your pardon," the Captain meekly apologized.

Sally sluffed a diamond in dummy and ruffed in hand with the six. "I'm just taking what's mine before y'all come after me," she announced glumly. Well, as you can readily see, what was hers turned out to be the balance of the tricks. Once she began running her clubs, not only did her diamond loser vanish but her trump loser as well. For if Penelope were to ruff the eight of clubs at trick nine, Sally would overruff, gather in the delinquent King of spades, enter dummy with the diamond King and jettison her nine of diamonds on the good club six. And if Gumpers were to let the third club go—as actually happened at table—McGonigle could pitch her losing diamond then and there, postponing the decapitation of the "guarded" trump King until the penultimate trick. Sure enough, upon the lead of the diamond King from dummy at trick twelve, Penelope was compelled to cough up either her King or her eight of trumps while Sally only had to puzzle out the appropriate order in which to play her Ace and her nine. "Wow!" she said, beaming with incredulity. "I guess you don't need thirty-three points for a baby slam after all!"

Piper shook his head from side to side and unleased a devilish grin. "Very nicely played, Miss Sally. Very nicely indeed."

"Hold on, now," Penelope protested. "Let's give credit where credit is due. She'd never've been able to reduce her trumps for the coup if Kane here hadn't obliged by leading a heart at the seventh trick." (The discriminating reader will notice how the woman's professed know-nothingism is thoroughly gainsaid by this remark.)

"Well, shoot," said Sally, "all I know is it's a good thing we played the hand in six spades instead of five hearts."

"Right you are, sweetie," groused Gumpers. "There's no way my partner could've bailed you out of that one."

44

Episode IV

In Which Diggery Performs the Soho Strip...
(November 15, 1982)

Looking back on that six-spade hand, I can see how Piper used bridge as a smoke screen. How he took advantage of Sally's atrocious play to throw me and everyone else off the track. For example, what preoccupied me that night (and several days thereafter, I must confess) was not the strange conversation during which Sally McGonigle balked at our mutual friend Reginald's name, but her ridiculous slam contract. This case of selective perception only goes to show, I suppose, how ill prepared we are to see in our everyday experience anything except that which it gives us no trouble or pain to comprehend. The more unlikely the coincidence or the more glaring the anomaly, the more willing we seem to be to take such phenomena at face value—to overlook discrepancies, to rationalize contradictions, to reconcile the irreconcilable.

For far too long during this Piper affair, I led the heedless, soporific existence against which Plato's Socrates, Voltaire's Candide and Bellow's Charlie Citrine all warned us. That unexamined life. That best of all possible worlds. That decades-long sleep of the soul. Yet sweet enlightenment came to me, reader. Not as it

45

came to Paul, perhaps, in a blinding burst of luminescence, but as it was accustomed to come to Poirot—in fitful flashes, disconnected by time and space. So it may be that by the fourth time Diggery showed up at the club, I had at least begun to stir from my deep slumber. But the day of my full awakening was not yet at hand. There is no denying the fact that at the time I met the cryptic Diggery Piper and listened to his Bicentennial tale, then welcomed Sally McGonigle back from her trip overseas and heard her stumble over her co-worker's name, then watched Sally and the Captain form a fast association at first sight—back when all those things happened I accepted each event as noteworthy in its own right but as completely unrelated to the others. But all that was back in the days of sloth and shadow. How well have I since learned the lesson that it is the luxury of children and fools to believe that things are what they seem.

The incident I have chosen to report from the club's November 15 session involves a heart-rending hand, and one which confirms the above-mentioned caveat regarding appearance versus reality. It is a hand in which care and precaution are repudiated, and rashness is bountifully rewarded; a hand during which the Congressional Duplicate Bridge Club's jealously guarded reputation for dignity and respectability was grievously besmirched, owing to the performance of a vulgar burlesque; a hand, in sum, in which your diarist rejected a simplistic (albeit effective) defense against a quixotic contract, engineered an infinitely more imaginative line and, for his pains, was force-fed another dose of Piper poison.

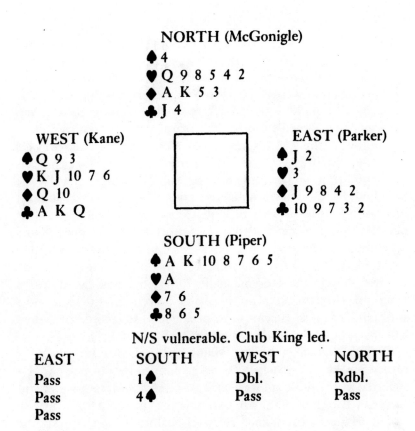

NORTH (McGonigle)

♠ 4
♥ Q 9 8 5 4 2
♦ A K 5 3
♣ J 4

WEST (Kane)

♠ Q 9 3
♥ K J 10 7 6
♦ Q 10
♣ A K Q

EAST (Parker)

♠ J 2
♥ 3
♦ J 9 8 4 2
♣ 10 9 7 3 2

SOUTH (Piper)

♠ A K 10 8 7 6 5
♥ A
♦ 7 6
♣ 8 6 5

N/S vulnerable. Club King led.

EAST	SOUTH	WEST	NORTH
Pass	1♠	Dbl.	Rdbl.
Pass	4♠	Pass	Pass
Pass			

It was the first freezing night of the winter. Snow fell against the windows of the Jefferson Lounge and settled thickly in the lower left corner of each pane. Across Constitution Avenue on the Capitol ellipse, where icicles hung from the beeches and elms, pedestrians could be seen fastening the collar buttons of their woolen coats and leaning stoically into the bitter northeast wind. Watching this scene from table four, a yard or so distant from the club's raging fireplace, I felt for a fleeting moment like Tolstoy's Pierre—protected from the tundra's bleak horrors by nothing more substantial than the gossamer cocoon of privilege.

The time was 9:30 P.M. and I was seated across from the Congressional's perennially reigning champion, Major Winthrop "Buttergut"Parker—the Pentagon liaison with the House Ap-.

47

propriations Committee. Parker was not called Buttergut for no-thing. He was a man of Brobdingnagian girth and, from all appearances, proud of it. For at the crucial moment of every bridge hand that went in his favor—and there were far more that did than that didn't—the Major invariably took to patting and caressing that fabled tummy with broad, proprietary strokes.

Another of the Major's more noticeable characteristics was his apparent inability to thrive without resorting to military patterns of locomotion, gesturing and speech. He did not walk, he marched. He did not shake hands or relax, he saluted and stood at ease. All of his turns were tidy quarters, halves or fulls. And half of what the man said had the ring of orders being shouted to a subordinate, while the other half seemed to be a nervous reaction that took the form of all but imperceptible mumbling. But if you listened closely, as I occasionally did, what you heard was a compulsive repetition of monosyllabic march-rhythm calls and a sprinkling of those salacious bits of doggerel so favored by sailors and marines ("Oh, I know a girl in Katmandu . . .").

"What's that, mister?" the Major had barked to me two days earlier on the phone when I'd asked him to be my partner. I'd repeated my request, adding "sir" at the end, and, to my pleasant surprise, had gotten a crisp "Affirmative" in reply.

The Major had remained relatively calm during the first nine boards of our game that evening. But now that we had forged a good hour and a half into the night's pressure-filled competition, and now that the table we were due to play at was Diggery's (whom, it became obvious to me, Buttergut had long since branded as a possible pretender to the club championship crown), he quickly retreated behind the cover of his infantryman persona. "HUT, hut, HUT, hut," Parker muttered, half to himself, as he marched on the Piper/McGonigle position. "HUT, hut, HUT, hut . . ."

"Evenin', Major," said Sally, who sat North.

"ONE, two, three, four, ONE . . ."

"Major," she continued, undaunted, "I want you to meet my new partner, Captain Diggery Piper."

"Actually, Miss Sally, the Major and I have already had the pleasure of..."

"SIR!" snapped Parker, executing a straight-backed, heel-clicking salute before suddenly taking his seat. He then dug himself in behind the thirteen cards of the East hand I showed you and began muttering a series of orders and exhortations that held no meaning for any but his own fevered mind. Rave on, I said to myself, for it was my theory that far from hindering his performance at table, that gibberish actually improved the man's concentration. I knew I had a better chance of teaching Piper a lesson with Buttergut Parker across from me than with any other player in the club.

Matters got off to a rather poor start when Diggery and Sally, that comely vision of blind luck incarnate, forced their way to game over my seventeen points. I call your attention, by the way, to Miss McGonigle's savvy redouble—the first of her life. For three nights following the Gerber-garbling incident of the previous Monday, Piper had schooled his partner in the fundamentals of Standard American bidding, one of the choicer fruits of which instruction is here displayed.

Once South's four spades was passed out I led the club King and noted Buttergut's play of the two. "Take the trump four off dummy," I could fairly hear that deuce scream. But I could hardly expect the Major (or perhaps even you, dear reader, lolling in the comfort of your armchair with all four hands in view) to appreciate my predicament. Who, I ask you (not counting Sally, of course), would lightly lead from the guarded trump Queen into the teeth of a presumed Ace-King-Jack combination just to scotch a third-round club ruff which declarer may not even need? Why trade one good trick for another at best or, should declarer have started with fewer than three clubs, for a phantom? Now, I wholeheartedly agree that your average bridge enthusiast should put less stock in inductive reasoning than in time-proven guidelines and techniques. But the superior player, I have always maintained, simply cannot permit himself to be shackled by the dictates of ironclad rules.

With this last thought in mind I bravely pushed the heart Jack, which was taken by Piper's Ace. When he came right back at me with another club, I turned to him with a smile and —I now admit it—grossly overstepped my bounds. "No use trying to coax out a trump shift," I chided him. "I didn't fall into the trap the first time and I'm not about to fall into it now. You see, I'm on to your subtle machinations."

"Come again?" Piper replied with what struck me as a cloying show of innocence.

"It would be just like you to sit there with two clubs and act like a man with three. (Parker, during all of this, kept babbling to himself, as if exiled in a private world.)... Well, I'm playing it safe. You're not gypping me out of my Queen." And here, knowing that East and South were both void of hearts, I led the six of that suit, never suspecting that a spade, a diamond, or strangely enough, a third club would have sealed the Captain's doom. My six brought a hopeful Queen from dummy and, from Buttergut, the trump Jack—a card which for very different reasons caught Diggery and me both by surprise. For he had not expected to run into a five-one heart break while I had not thought I'd find so key a trump card in my partner's hand.

My first reaction was one of remorse at not having smothered dummy's spade as I'd been instructed, for it immediately became clear that Diggery had not been perpetrating a ruse at all but had been playing straightforwardly for a club ruff. A trump shift at trick two or four would have let us take three clubs and a trump for down one. Yet I soon realized that what had not been done with a bludgeon had perhaps been done with a stiletto. When the Captain was forced to cover that insidious spade Jack with his Ace, I saw that Parker had redeemed me with an uppercut. Instead of a third club and a trump, I would now rake in two trumps. In my excitement I tabled my spade holding and unloaded a burden of pent-up frustration.

"Here," said I, "let me save you some time. My Queen-nine-three of trumps lies behind your King-ten."

"Oh, my," said Sally McGonigle, upon whom not all things were lost.

50

"So it does," said Buttergut Parker with a new-found calmness in his voice. I noticed too that he'd begun stroking the upper half of his massive stomach, which secured the edge of the table like a vise.

"You see, I must get two trump tricks," I spelled out for Diggery, who seemed reluctant to concede the obvious. "You're down one, my friend."

"Not," said he, "if you happen to be holding what I think you're holding."

"Oh, brother," warned Sally. "Hold on to your sombreros, cause here we go again!"

Piper ("...lest the defense should labor under the slightest disadvantage") now splayed his nine remaining cards on the tabletop at this juncture:

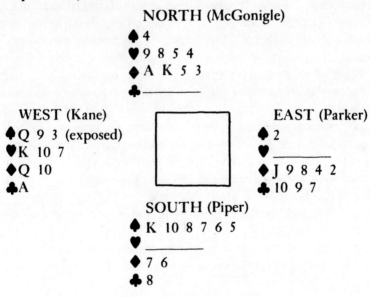

NORTH (McGonigle)
♠ 4
♥ 9 8 5 4
♦ A K 5 3
♣ ———

WEST (Kane)
♠ Q 9 3 (exposed)
♥ K 10 7
♦ Q 10
♣ A

EAST (Parker)
♠ 2
♥ ———
♦ J 9 8 4 2
♣ 10 9 7

SOUTH (Piper)
♠ K 10 8 7 6 5
♥ ———
♦ 7 6
♣ 8

He then cautioned Sally to avert her gaze. "The stratagem to which I find I must now resort," he explained, "is hardly fit for a lady's eyes."

"What's it called?" Sally asked.

"The Soho Strip," was his candid reply. And for the first time in our month-long acquaintance, I saw the Captain blush. Sally's cheeks colored as well, and after uttering an involuntary exclamation, she turned her hazel eyes floorward and waited in shocked silence. This was hardly the reaction of Winthrop Parker, who neither blushed nor turned away. On the contrary, his face ran white as he gawked at all those upturned cards, and his right hand froze on the northernmost reaches of his belly.

"Show time!" announced Diggery. There then ensued a performance of the most lurid nature; one which threatened to undo in a trice the unsullied tradition of propriety which it had taken the Congressional Bridge Club membership a good twenty-six years to build. First he sashayed to dummy with a diamond and ambled back to his hand via a heart ruff. Then he repeated that shameful routine, thereby peeling my side-suit protection down to a scanty heart and club. Next he set about bumping the latter by ruffing his club eight in dummy, and grinding my heart suit down to nothing with a final ruff in hand. "Are you ready for the show-stopper?" he teased. I was sitting there now stripped of all but the Queen-nine-three of trumps, which still lay face up on the table. When Piper played low from his King-ten-eight, my embarrassment was complete.

I was momentarily dazed. My cards were no more than a blur before me. Far in the background I could vaguely hear the Major hut-hutting his way toward the coffee buffet.

"Can I look now?" asked Sally, whose eyes were still riveted to the lounge's carpet.

"Yes," Diggery replied, smoothing down the ruffles of his shirtfront. "Yes, Miss Sally, you may look. And let what you see be a lesson to you—to wit, a man who somehow managed in one fell swoop both to pull the wool over his own eyes and to end up with not a stitch on."

Episode V

In Which Sally Unveils the McGonigle Coup...
(December 27, 1982)

It is nine in the morning here on my promenade bench. My spirits are high, for the smog has at long last cleared away and the writing progresses apace. I will meet my deadline, I know. Already I feel free enough to indulge in an occasional distraction, like watching one of the great ships from Europe or Asia as it steams down the mouth of the river toward the docks. Or gazing at a freak occurrence in that deep cerulean sky—the sun climbing steeply in the east as, in the west, the pallid specter of a full moon still remains. The experience, at first entrancing, quickly palls, for I am reminded of the last time I witnessed such a sight. It was at 6:45 P.M., November 20 of last year, as I was strolling home from a long day of work at the mailroom. It was the evening I became officially unattached.

Jane, I hasten to point out, was blameless. With a batch of month-old bridge quarrels still fermenting in her mind and with the prospect of yet another sleepless night ahead (I had not purposely wakened her the two Mondays before, but the twin specter of Sally's six-spade disaster and Piper's Soho Strip had caused me such torment that the springs of the mattress creaked all night long), Jane presented me with a reasonable ultimatum: either I was to bid farewell to bridge or she was to bid farewell to me.

As I feel the impartial reader will readily admit, my bridge life soon developed complications that fully justified, on moral and patriotic grounds, my persevering with the game. But the sick compulsion that prevented me from canceling at least the next week's club date is something I will never understand. Perhaps, as Jane held, I had become a card addict and could no longer function without my Monday-night fix. Perhaps I was being driven by some pitiful need to humble Diggery just once and so to restore my self-respect. Whatever the reason, I was unable to abstain from my masochistic diversion, and so lost for a time the one person who, I know, could make me happy. I say "for a time" not because we have since reunited. (As you have known from the start of this journal, I am still involved in bridge; and Jane's strength of will is such that there is no chance of her relenting on this point.) No, I use that sanguine phrase only because I have every intention of prostrating myself before her and begging that she take me back...once the cursed chain of victories to be chronicled in a later section of this diary is at long last severed.

But enough of my plans for the future. It is time I returned to the task at hand.

Much to the dismay of the more established members of the Congressional Duplicate Bridge Club (and I certainly count myself among that number), the seemingly chance pairing of Diggery Piper and Sally McGonigle soon blossomed into a redoubtable partnership. Week after week the club's acclaimed experts teamed up in a concerted effort to pierce that unlikely duo's armor of genuine skill and dumb luck, and week after week they failed. Some of our less scrupulous members even began smuggling in ringers as guests—at first a few bridge bums lured from their tony Chevy Chase country clubs by the promise of plump retainers, then circuit-seasoned pros drawn from as far away as New York City.

And yet the outcome never varied. Sometimes Sally and the

Captain took first by a smattering of points, sometimes by a bundle. But they always took first.

The following hand, with the bidding purposely excluded, is taken from a session played in late December. It demonstrates the flexibility, shall we say, of the Piper/McGonigle style:

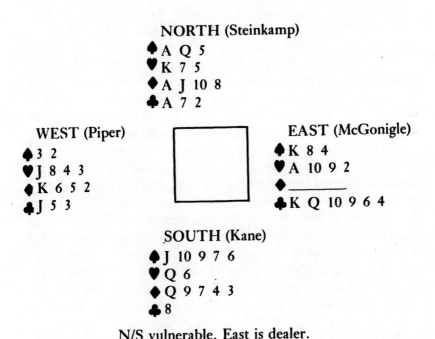

NORTH (Steinkamp)
♠ A Q 5
♥ K 7 5
♦ A J 10 8
♣ A 7 2

WEST (Piper)
♠ 3 2
♥ J 8 4 3
♦ K 6 5 2
♣ J 5 3

EAST (McGonigle)
♠ K 8 4
♥ A 10 9 2
♦ _____
♣ K Q 10 9 6 4

SOUTH (Kane)
♠ J 10 9 7 6
♥ Q 6
♦ Q 9 7 4 3
♣ 8

N/S vulnerable. East is dealer.

I have chosen to include this pearl in my collection because it gives the lie to an assumption that the reader may, quite understandably, have made by now: namely, that Sally and Diggery's stock in trade lay almost exclusively in the area of offense. And further, that their *modus operandi* generally required the one to distract all opposing teams with her auburn tresses, sparkling eyes and totally arbitrary bidding techniques while the other effortlessly extricated himself from the preposterous contracts into which his cohort invariably plunged him.

Not so. The mischief that pair caused was in no way restricted to the offense. The above hand, which months ago worked its way into the club's unwritten mythology, proves that Miss McGonigle's unnerving blend of ineptitude and wide-eyed luck prevailed regardless of who was declarer.

I recall that in my desperation that night, I demeaned myself. In the seven weeks that had elapsed since I'd been unceremoniously dumped by the Captain, I had gone through seven new partners, each condescending to play with me no more than a single session. It may have been mere coincidence or, since I always seemed to net zero to five out of a possible twenty-four matchpoints when competing at Diggery's table, I may have been branded as some kind of jinx. In any case Reginald Graves—whom I regarded as my regular partner now that Jane had abandoned me—was not due back in the country before the following Tuesday, and I'd exhausted my list of worthy substitutes.

And so, in order to avoid the stigma of being paired by our partnership coordinator with some chippie just up from the novice ranks, I swallowed my pride and approached the club's eighty-three-year-old dean, former Senator Richard A. Steinkamp of Nebraska. After serving for nearly fifty-four years as chairman of the Senate Subcommittee on Tidal Wave Control and birddogging the annual $2,483 budget of the National Typhoon Preparedness Board, "Old Tight Fist," as his colleagues had long ago dubbed him, had built a reputation for frugality that stretched from one end of the Old Senate Office Building to the other.

"Senator," I'd said to him earlier that night, momentarily forgetting that he'd always dismissed hearing aids as extravagances. "Senator? SENATOR?"

"What's that? What? Oh, Kane. Should know better than to sneak up on a fellow that way."

"Sorry, Senator."

"Well, what's on your mind? Speak up, son."

"I need a par——I mean, I wanted to know if you'd be interested in playing with me as your partner tonight. I was thinking earlier this week that it's been quite a long time since you and I have sat across from each..."

"Already got someone in mind for a partner," snapped Steinkamp in the tart, laconic style that has always been his trademark.

"You do?" Then I drew nearer to the man and pitched my voice at a level at which I hoped I could make myself heard by the Senator but not by the dozens of club members who were milling about the lounge. "Perhaps," I said, "perhaps we could work out some arrangement."

"What kind of an arrangment?" he inquired with the type of blood-curdling shout of which the near-deaf so often avail themselves.

"Please, Senator, if you would just lower your..."

"Cost you the price of my entry," he blared. When I looked around nervously, half the players in the room were staring in our direction.

"Done," said I before retreating in mortal shame to the anonymity of the Congressional washroom.

The first few rounds went reasonably well that night. Outside of having to repeat a number of my bids two or three times for the Senator's benefit, I had very few problems with my new partner. Although his was not the most compatible temperament to deal with, Old Tight Fist was now as stingy with a bridge trick as he had been in his glory years with John Q. Public's dollar. I knew that if I but brought to that session my usual competence and circumspection, we were a shoo-in to place in the standings.

We were spared Piper and McGonigle until round four. When the Captain arrived at our table he bid the Senator good evening twice before realizing that he was not destined to be heard, then pulled the West cards from their compartment and waited until his partner announced the zany opening you see recorded below (now that you have had a chance to bid the hand rationally, reader, I re-present it along with the calls that were actually made), then sat back self-satisfied to await developments...

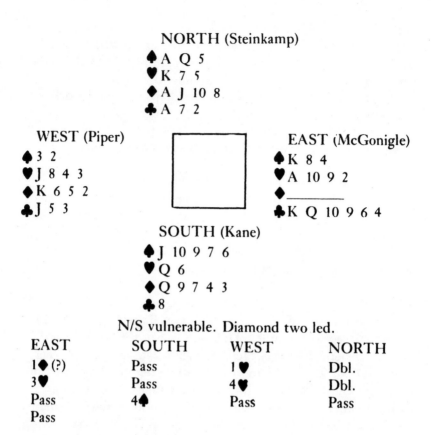

NORTH (Steinkamp)
♠ A Q 5
♥ K 7 5
♦ A J 10 8
♣ A 7 2

WEST (Piper)
♠ 3 2
♥ J 8 4 3
♦ K 6 5 2
♣ J 5 3

EAST (McGonigle)
♠ K 8 4
♥ A 10 9 2
♦ _____
♣ K Q 10 9 6 4

SOUTH (Kane)
♠ J 10 9 7 6
♥ Q 6
♦ Q 9 7 4 3
♣ 8

N/S vulnerable. Diamond two led.

EAST	SOUTH	WEST	NORTH
1♦ (?)	Pass	1♥	Dbl.
3♥	Pass	4♥	Dbl.
Pass	4♠	Pass	Pass
Pass			

I passed, only to hear Piper respond, my partner double and
Sally make a jump rebid in hearts. Again I passed. But when
Diggery pressed on to game and Steinkamp doubled once more, I
was convinced that some serious point shading was going on. Nor
was it difficult to finger the probable culprit. As far as anyone
knew, the parsimonious Senator had never made an overbid in
several decades at table while Diggery, in the ten weeks during
which he had graced our company, had seldom made anything
but. (Sally's bids, of course, were consistent only in their unpre-
dictability and, on the issue of accuracy, rarely repaid serious
conjecture—a fact I might have done well to keep in mind during
this particular incident.)

I decided, therefore, that Piper was merely snatching at a

58

bargain-priced sacrifice. And so, trusting my intuition and the bone-crusher promised by my partner's two vulnerable doubles, I went ahead and hazarded a game bid in spades.

"Thankee, thankee," I exlaimed as the lead of the diamond two came down and Tight Fist tabled his splendid hand, for I was exulting in the precision of my judgment. We figured to put their doubled four hearts down two tricks at best for a score of 300, while four spades—at least the way I was ready to play it—was virtually a laydown.

How well I knew the terrain. Had I not, after all, seen variations of this theme in scores of Truscott, Goren and Sheinwold columns? Was I not intimately familiar with the fate of the greedy South who disregards the bidding and lunges at the finesse at trick one, only to watch with horror as East plays the King and gives West the ruff that ultimately defeats the contract?

Not for me the pedestrian diamond hook. Not for me that bush-league sucker play. Sure, I knew from her first bid that it was Sally and not Diggery who held the King. But how much more I knew! Counting the lead, my five and dummy's four, I could see ten diamonds from where I sat. *Ergo*, Sally must have bid that suit holding the King-six-five. One glance at her convention card informed me that she and Diggery were using the "better minor" method of bidding weak, balanced openings, so I knew for a certainty not only that she held no five-card major but that she had been dealt fewer than four clubs as well. Now, I admit it did not take a genius to envision her hand as something along the order of:

♠K x x		♠K x x x
♥A x x x	or	♥A x x x
♦K x x		♦K x x
♣Q x x		♣K x

but I was nonetheless pleased with my analysis.

Furthermore, whichever of those two possible distributions she held in her hands (Sally has always been one of those players who clutch their cards in both fists, as if someone were threatening to take them away), I was more than ready for her. The key, of course, is to rise immediately with the diamond Ace, eschewing the futile finesse, and to follow right up with the Ace of trumps, spurning the highly unpromising spade hook as well. Now the surrender of a spade ensures that West—who, given the unassailability of the above bidding analysis, had to start with either one spade or two—has been voided of trumps with which to ruff diamonds, and so deprives the defense of its setting trick. Nothing spectacular, really. Just a marriage of two safety plays clearly indicated by the bidding.

I called for the diamond Ace and calmly regarded Sally's play of the trump four as one of her endearing revokes. I smiled, perhaps a tad patronizingly, and permitted Piper to acquaint his partner with the custom of following suit.

"Miss Sally," he said in the reverential tone with which he always addressed her, "you really must play a diamond."

"Shoot, I would if I had one," she said, "but I don't." It was at this point that I began to experience genuine concern.

"What do you mean, you don't?" I screamed. "You bid them, didn't you?"

"Heck, no. I bid one club and three hearts. Why in tarnation would I go and bid a suit I'm plumb out of?"

"Whose turn to play?" growled Steinkamp, visibly peeved by this delay. But I sat paralyzed, unable even to complete that first trick.

Now, there cannot be one member of the Congressional Duplicate Bridge Club who has ever derived pleasure from receiving a bottom board at the hands of Diggery Piper. Yet at least there is no shame in losing to a player of such skill. It is when the blow is delivered by the fairer half of the Piper/McGonigle partnership that one's blood tends to boil; and never more hotly than when the awkward machinery of Sally's blind fortune is laid unmercifully bare. Which is exactly what the Captain now proceeded to do.

"Gentlemen," he intoned with Mephistophelian glee, "I know this tactic well. It came up once in last Monday night's game and twice last month. 'The McGonigle Coup,' as I have named it, is a bidding stratagem of surpassing delicacy—an unconscious, lead-directing psyche, to be exact. Once Miss Sally has duly misdescribed her hand by bidding a suit she does not happen to possess, her innocent partner, suffering under the delusion that he is merely leading to her strength, unwittingly induces declarer to make the one play that puts the contract out of reach..."

"Oh, no," I muttered. "Oh, no."

"...If, for example, you had called for any diamond but the Ace here, Terence, I dare say your spade game would have been unbeatable, even granting the first-trick ruff. That's just the way this extraordinary gambit seems to operate. Offhand I'd guess that the loss sustained at trick one would later have been recouped through repeated finesses against my by then marked diamond King. Am I close?"

I chose not to give him the satisfaction of hearing just how close he was.

"Now wait a minute," Steinkamp whined, having finally understood that he was being deprived of something he regarded as his due. "That one-diamond bid is unethical."

"Not," the Captain hastened to point out, "if the bidder doesn't know what in God's name she's... Not, that is to say, if one is entirely unaware of one's oversight."

Once the injury had been inflicted—the loss of a spade, a heart, a diamond and the ruff put me down one—there remained only the insult. Naturally, Sally obliged. Unable to leave well enough alone, she scooped up the Captain's cards, scrutinized his holding and shook her head accusingly from side to side. "Why in glory'd you bid those weak ol' hearts when you could've supported my clubs? We had nine of them between us, you know."

"You're quite right, of course," Diggery replied. "I assure you, Miss Sally, it's a mistake I shan't make twice."

Episode VI

In Which Diggery Demonstrates the Force of Parrot Power...

(January 3, 1983)

If I have discovered one thing in the course of writing this journal, if there is one fresh fact I can add to the store of my narrow experience, it is the per-hour rate at which a given number of sea gulls can be counted on to pelt a stationary target. Do not furrow your brows in disbelief, you who are used to jogging along ocean beaches, bobbing about in the surf or lying on the sand under your gaily striped (and, I would wager, thickly encrusted) umbrellas. You have your constant movement, the volatile ocean winds, your canvas shields to protect you. But I have nothing. I sit in the open, moving not an inch, as the hours pass by. And *they* come, swarming down on me like dive bombers with the blinding sun at their backs and shrieking with predatory delight. Then, with frightening regularity (if I may use that word), they keep reminding me of their presence in ways other than the visual or aural.

Would that that were the only discomfiture those spiteful creatures caused me. But it is not. No, they remind me, as well, of a night at the club when I engaged in hand-to-pinion combat with that poor excuse for a mascot never found very far from Diggery Piper's right ear. You may take it on faith that when compared with Hermione, these gulls are a study in ornithological decorum.

If the truth must be told, I never could understand how in spite of the obvious sanitary problems, in spite of the raucous squawking (which I was once gullible enough to believe was the random noise production of a witless bird), in spite of the questionable protocol of admitting an unruly, exotic animal within the hallowed halls of Congress—how in spite of all this, Diggery's parrot was permitted to perch week after week on her master's shoulder and stare in avian insolence at the hands he so deftly played. Until the third of January I had taken it for granted that the Captain's despicable pet contributed in no way to his uncanny success at table, and so never formally protested its presence. But that evening I gained sufficient evidence to disprove this naive assumption.

And the shame of it is, that Monday night could so easily have been a joyous, even festive, occasion. For just when it appeared I would have to undergo the aforementioned ignominy of registering at the partnership desk (Old Tight Fist himself, I knew, was prepared to play that night with anyone but me, even if it meant he had to pay for his own entry), who should show up but Reginald Graves, back a day early from his research assignment abroad.

Reginald, you see, understood me. He knew how much of my free time I devoted to the game. How I'd read everything from Goren to Garozzo on bidding, everything from Kelsey to Kantar on defense, and how I could quote page-long sections from Reese and Dormer's *Complete Book of Bridge* and from Watson's *Play of the Hand*. He understood that there are those in life who suffer from congenital bad fortune and that I, alas, was so afflicted. He understood the agony I experienced session after session in continually falling victim to a disproportionate share of abominable trump breaks, in being dealt so many hands that proved to be exceptions to book play, in losing out week after week to demonstrably inferior competition. All of this Reginald understood.

And for the first hour or so it appeared that the two of us had somehow managed to pick up right where we'd left off the previous September. I'd scored our first fifteen hands as seven absolute

63

tops, seven absolute bottoms and one average plus. Furthermore our play was free, as in the old days, of the tiresome fault-finding and bickering so characteristic of less mature partnerships.

That spirit of well-being and camaraderie lasted until round six, when it came time to play three boards with Sally and the Captain and, I feel compelled to add, with Hermione. I introduced Reginald to Diggery, who complimented my friend on his elegant Halston tie, and everything went smoothly until Reginald began extolling the beauty of southern Bahrein. It was then that Sally McGonigle said, "Sounds real nice. You know, it seems to me I've heard of that place." At this extraordinary pronouncement, Piper and Graves exchanged a horrified glance—a glance which did not escape my notice.

"But I thought you were there yourself just two and a half months ago," I said, confused by this blatant discrepancy. "As a matter of fact, I thought the staffs of the House Foreign Affairs and Senate Foreign Relations committees had worked together in Bahrein during the month of..."

"We did, we did!" Reginald hastened to interject. "Remember, Sally, back in October? The undulating dunes, the colorful tents, the gaunt Arab sheiks in their..."

"Oh...oh, were you boys talking about Bay-Rhine? I...I thought you said something like Bah-Rain."

"Ah, that explains it," said Piper with a nervous laugh, so out of character for him. "A simple case of mistaken identity. Miss Sally pronounces the place name one way while Mr. Graves pronounces it another. That certainly accounts for the mix-up."

"Sure," I said tentatively. "Sure it does."

The three of them made as if the incident were completely forgotten. I too played along for the time being. But even though I lay low and neglected to act for several hours on what I had learned, my mind—on a subconscious level at least—was arranging and rearranging what I finally realized were the interconnected pieces of a puzzle.

When we turned at last to bridge it was with a commonly shared sense of relief, for the game offered a convenient respite from the

64

palpable, if unavowed, tension. In no time at all things appeared to return (and I stress the word "appeared") to business as usual.

Nothing of consequence occurred during the first two hands. Sally did bid out of turn on one and lead out of turn on the other, but neither of these contretemps seemed to have affected the outcome. The deal you see before you, however, is of another ilk entirely:

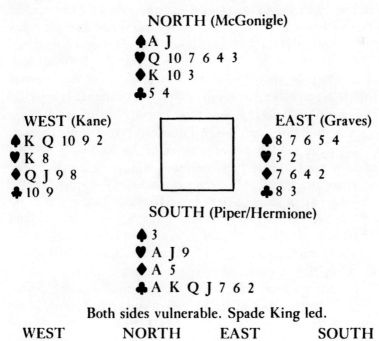

NORTH (McGonigle)
♠ A J
♥ Q 10 7 6 4 3
♦ K 10 3
♣ 5 4

WEST (Kane)
♠ K Q 10 9 2
♥ K 8
♦ Q J 9 8
♣ 10 9

EAST (Graves)
♠ 8 7 6 5 4
♥ 5 2
♦ 7 6 4 2
♣ 8 3

SOUTH (Piper/Hermione)
♠ 3
♥ A J 9
♦ A 5
♣ A K Q J 7 6 2

Both sides vulnerable. Spade King led.

WEST	NORTH	EAST	SOUTH
1♠	2♥	Pass	4NT
Pass	5♦	Pass	7NT
Dbl.	Pass	Pass	Pass

I opened in the West seat with one spade. Please do not think for a moment that I was unaware of my lamentable dearth of Aces. But reverberating in my brain were the counsels of such mentors as Roth and Schenken and Kaplan and Frey, relating to the favorable grouping of honors, the utility of sturdy intermediates and the preemptive power of a five-card spade suit. Well, the obstructive value of my opening proved to be less than over-whelming when the irrepressible McGonigle promptly overcalled with a jaunty two hearts. Reginald took one look at the dross he'd been dealt and passed.

Now Diggery must have brightened inwardly at Sally's vulner-able overcall before adequately considering its source. In any event, he launched into Blackwood and uncovered the one card he felt he still needed for the grand slam—the spade Ace. (He was already counting on his partner to hold a five- or six-card heart suit headed at the very least by the King, if not by both missing honors.) Once he found what he was looking for he rocketed straight to seven notrump, seven hearts being summarily rejected on the basis that it would install the "wrong" hand as declarer.

Imagine the relish with which I doubled this absurd contract. After all, I did hold stoppers in three of the four suits. (And I mention parenthetically that once the dummy appeared, every one of those guards, including the suspect heart King, took on the consistency of tempered steel.) Even if Reginald held a hand from which the Second Earl of Yarborough might have cringed—and his eight-high surely qualifies—we would still be sure to reap a juicy top. Predictably enough, Diggery's face turned a delightful shade of sepulchral gray as my spade King and Sally's dummy floated in tandem to the table. But I will give him this much credit. He braced up in the face of certain defeat and smiled wanly in his partner's direction.

"Thank you, Miss Sally," he murmured. At times like these his formal graciousness has always struck me as particularly touch-ing.

"I hope it's what you expected, Captain."

"It is that and more, my dear." Piper stared and stared at his cards before playing to the first trick, which was so unlike his usual practice of running roughshod over the defense with nary a moment's hesitation.

After sitting through two full minutes of such cogitating I

finally succumbed to temptation. "You might as well just play it out and take your lumps," I taunted. "Not even the gods of bridge could get you out of this mess."

"Perhaps not," he replied, the break in the silence seeming to jolt him from a trance. "But Hermione probably could."

"Not the parrot?" I asked incredulously. I should have played it safe. Oh, how I wish I'd kept quiet then. Chalked up the profit we would have gained if Piper had been left to his own devices. Squirreled away one tasty victory against a bitter season of defeats. But no, I felt as expansive as I did confident. "Feel free," I offered, "to make any use you wish of that sullen beast."

At these unfortunate words the Captain shrugged his right shoulder, sending Hermione in flight and throwing the Congressional Club members into a collective dither. Senator Winfield dropped her cards in astonishment; Congressman Fishley took a wild swipe at the bird with his walking stick; Heinrich Hemholz, that grizzled martinet who keeps the Speaker's office purring like a well-oiled diesel, appeared to choke momentarily on his pipe stem. Every eye was trained on Hermione as she circled our table in a dramatic, hawklike swoop before descending once again to her lookout.

Piper waited patiently for the commotion to cease. Then, peering in mock insouciance at his anemic eleven-trick holding, announced, "I believe I am now prepared to play out this hand." He called for the spade Ace and pointed toward the hearts in dummy. But just as I was fondly contemplating the doomed heart hook, the rapid-fire spade plays and the delivery of a tart 1400-point sting, Hermione squawked.

"What on earth is the matter?" Diggery asked her. "I might just as well hazard the heart finesse now as later. Let's face up to it, we're in for either a top or a bottom. And where else but in hearts can I hope to collect the two tricks I'm short?"

Again the parrot raved, now emitting an alternate series of nasal and sibilant sounds which, to my ears at least, bore an ungodly resemblance to the phrase: "Offside! Offside!"

"Well, just to humor you I'll postpone the play for now," the Captain allowed. "But mind you, I don't see any prospect of

67

avoiding it." With the pained look of a slave compelled to do his master's bidding, Piper began peeling off his seven club tricks. Only then did the parrot's warnings take on an eerie sense of menace. Suddenly the placement of dummy's spade Jack over my Queen struck me as vaguely unsettling; my protected King of hearts no longer *felt* protected; and the Queen-Jack of diamonds became barer and barer as Diggery's endless club winners cut into my once mighty store of stoppers. In the end I divested myself of the diamond guard, unable to maintain a stranglehold on all three suits. I was secure after all in the knowledge that even if Piper were to euchre me out of one trick, he would still have only twelve available. He and Sally would post a minus score while all the other North/South pairs would be bidding and making six hearts. Besides, who could guess that I was down to the stiff Queen-Jack of diamonds?

The parrot, of course, could guess.

When Diggery mused aloud, "I think I'll go up to the dummy and take that heart finesse," the bird went berserk. At this point I called in our director, Mr. Gradys, and registered a formal complaint. Who would have done otherwise in my place?

There is one visual feature which immediately sets Edmund Gradys apart from most other mild-mannered fifty-year-old men of average build. That is a gruesome little bulge just to the left of his breastbone—a lump caused by the presence, twixt shirt and jacket, of *The Laws of Duplicate Contract Bridge*. He is reputed to tote this volume with him at all times—whether or not he happens to be officiating at a game. The compilation of rules and proprieties, lashed into its custom-made leather holster, gives Gradys the appearance of a benign hit man.

It is my opinion that Edmund's reputation for fairness and diplomacy were irreparably tarnished that evening. I invite you to judge for yourself. He stood at our table and smiled down on us in silence. The fingers of his right hand, poised to riffle through that beloved mass of onionskin, were twitching with a gunslinger's anticipation.

"Declarer," I archly accused, "is making unwarranted use of information supplied to him by Hermione."

Edmund was visibly taken aback and I thought at first that I had won my case. "Shame on you, Terry," he scolded. "You've been a member of this club long enough to know Sally's name by now."

"I think you should cut your losses right here," Reginald advised me. And sound advice it was. But once I am launched on a course of action—above all one in which a question of principle is involved—I am not very easily deterred.

"I wasn't referring to his partner," I explained as patiently as I could. "I was referring to his bird."

"Come again?"

Sally whispered to Gradys at a volume level admirably suited to the typical Shakespearean aside, "He's upset that Captain Piper is finding out how to play this hand from the parrot..." Edmund did not appear to be particularly impressed by that piece of news. His right hand now hung listlessly at his side. "...But if I were you," she continued, "I'd refuse to rule that the use of the information is 'unwarranted.'"

"And I'll bet I know why," Reginald interrupted with a smile. "I'll bet you don't think it's unwarranted because Terry here said it would be all right if the Captain used the bird against us."

"Keerect!" said Sally.

Gradys smiled blandly. "Yes, well, there being no article in my rulebook dealing with the unwarranted use of parrots, you'll understand if I ask that play continue."

"But..."

"Without further delay." Edmund walked back toward the scorer's table, mumbling all the way about the good old days at the Cavendish Club.

Examine the position we had reached at trick nine and see the dire straits into which that blasted bird had steered me:

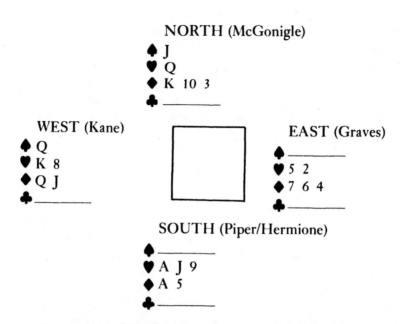

NORTH (McGonigle)
♠ J
♥ Q
♦ K 10 3
♣ ———

WEST (Kane)
♠ Q
♥ K 8
♦ Q J
♣ ———

EAST (Graves)
♠ ———
♥ 5 2
♦ 7 6 4
♣ ———

SOUTH (Piper/Hermione)
♠ ———
♥ A J 9
♦ A 5
♣ ———

With Hermione no doubt subtly guiding the proceedings, Piper once again spurned the heart finesse, instead playing out his Ace, King and ten of diamonds. And just as the final club had earlier embarrassed me for a discard in three suits, the final diamond now embarrassed me for a discard in two. This time I got to choose between promoting the spade Jack in dummy or baring my precious King of hearts. My face must have betrayed my chagrin.

"Let me put you out of your misery, my good man," Diggery said, "and at the same time lay your suspicions to rest..." (How rational, even helpful, Piper's analyses of his own brilliance had sounded back in the days when I was his partner, and he was directing them at some truly deserving victim. But how patronizing those *ex post facto* confections never failed to strike me when I myself was their target.) "...I never had any intention of taking the heart finesse," he had the gall to claim. "You see, your opening spade bid and subsequent double furnished me with a perfectly accurate idea of where to place the King-Queen of spades, the King of hearts and the Queen-Jack of diamonds, given the fact that Miss Sally's holding, when added to mine, left only eleven honor

70

points unaccounted for in the deck. Therefore the finesse amounted to certain suicide while the simple expedient of playing out my club winners until your guards wilted one by one seemed to be a rather jolly alternative, eh wot? Construct for yourself any distribution you wish and you will see that if West but holds those five critical face cards, he can never prevail. Your theorists label this play 'the progressive squeeze,'" he continued, shuffling his cards and replacing them in the container with a flourish, "although Hermione has coined her own phrase for the maneuver. I believe it describes the peculiar movement of a certain type of wrench. So much more apt an epithet, if you ask me..."

"I'm really not interested," I replied. But as I rose and trudged dejectedly toward table seven, the parrot rasped, "Ratchet! Ratchet!" for everyone to hear.

A Strange Interlude...

(January 4, 1983)

To the reader who brings to this journal nothing but the standard bridge player's insatiable lust for display after display of card combinations he has not yet seen, I say move on. Proceed directly to my entry of January 10. For this episode contains no deal, no bidding, no analysis of any end position; it will hold no interest for you whatsoever. And to the reader who has by now painted some private portrait of Diggery Piper as an eccentric, card-daffy Briton traipsing through America on extended holiday, to that reader I say lay this journal aside altogether. For in forging on, you will find that image, for all its quaintness and color, is bound to fade beyond recognition once it is placed in the harsh light of reality. But to those of you who admit the existence of a vast range of emotions and motivations inspired by matters other than bridge, and who have no predilection for being shielded from life as it is lived, to those readers I issue an invitation to join me on a journey—the journey I made through the city of Washington on the morning following Sally McGonigle's fumbling over the pronunciation of Bahrein. (No, I had not banished that telltale conversation from my consciousness but had merely salted it away for

72

solitary study.) The nature of that journey, as you may by now have guessed, was reconnaissance.

It is true that back in those days I still fell prey at table to an occasional Soho Strip or McGonigle Coup, or even to a parrot-operated Ratchet Squeeze. But at least I'd begun sensitizing myself to the most minuscule twists of plot in the larger theater of life. The proof of this awakening came during the night of January 3, when I reached the irrefutable conclusion that an intrigue was afoot—an intrigue involving three people I had thought of as friends. Needless to say I was determined at all costs to ascertain both its nature and scope.

Diggery, I knew, would be the key. And it was outside his Capitol Hill apartment building that I waited in hiding on the raw, cold morning of the fourth. (To find out where he lived, I'd simply checked the membership card which he'd been required to file with Nora Graham.) I'd phoned in sick earlier that morning; someone else would have to sort the Congressional mail that day. Beneath the pines and blue spruces of Folger Park I crouched from eight until ten, watching tenant after tenant leave the Bradley Arms at the corner of Second and D Streets, Southeast, and hustle off with attaché case and umbrella in hand toward the various House and Senate office buildings. The rain that had begun falling around 9:15 was as fine as mist and had not at first seemed strong enough even to penetrate my clothing. But in time the shoulders of my white London Fog were streaked gray and my ancient pair of hiking boots no longer proved impervious to moisture.

I was in fact on the point of retreating home for a hot bath when a dapper male figure stepped through the doorway I was watching, looked quickly up and down Second Street, then struck out west on D. He too carried an umbrella and briefcase but the continental cut of his suit and the presence of a stylish black derby distinguished him instantaneously from the others. At first the Van Dyke beard and relatively conservative clothing threatened to throw me off, but before he was even half a block away I was on

73

to the game. I was sure that this character was none other than Captain Diggery Piper.

My first reaction (do not laugh) was to assume not only that my paranoia had been vindicated but that I'd caught Piper right at the inception of his dastardly scheme—whatever it was. However, a moment's reflection led me to realize that this disguised trip into the city was in all probability just the latest in a series of clandestine forays.

Stealthily, oh, so stealthily, I stalked him from afar, using the trees and parked cars on the opposite side of the street to cover my pursuit, all the while keeping that initial half block of distance between us. No one but a trained actor, I once read, can so alter his manner of walking as to eliminate every trace of his accustomed gait and bearing. Here Piper was no exception. Although he attempted to conceal his graceful carriage by affecting a slight limp, each step he took further resolved any doubts I might still have entertained as to his identity.

Yet clearer still was the identity of the trench-coated individual who approached him at precisely 10:14 A.M., just before he reached the top step of the Capitol South subway escalator on First Street between C and D. It was not likely, after all, that I would mistake the tall, stocky form of the man with whom, for the better part of a year now, I had sat down to play bridge—barring, of course, his three-month trip to "Bay-Rhine." The two men crossed paths at right angles and said not a word to one another, Reginald continuing smoothly on toward the Rayburn Building and Diggery toward the metro. The exchange of identical beige leather satchels was swift, even expert, but once again clearly visible from my vantage point across the way. I was at a crossroads, but chose quickly to stick with the ringleader. How far I had come, I can remember thinking, from my sheltered university days, how far from the puerile concerns of Sibley High. Perhaps the trembling of my hand on the escalator railing as I doggedly tracked Piper underground was a measure of the shock I was experiencing then; the sensation of radical disorientation in the face of this mounting body of evidence.

74

The first clandestine contact, it pains me to report, proved no more than a prelude to even more baleful goings-on. Employing that method of subway pursuit most highly recommended by ex-OSS operative Filibert Rossignol in his controversial espionage manual, *The Compleat Spook*, I successfully tailed Diggery to Metro Center, where he transferred from the Blue to the Red Line, then on to the Dupont Circle station. There he ascended into the gray but now rainless daylight and headed across Massachusetts Avenue toward the park.

On a sunny day in any season, Dupont Circle—that broad, grassy oasis located at the traffic-ringed nexus of Connecticut, Massachusetts, New Hampshire, Nineteenth and P—is filled with street musicians, panhandlers, lunching bankers and diplomatic aides, drug dealers, plain-clothes policemen, socialist proselytizers, prostitutes, bug-eyed tourists, doomsday orators and a motley collection of chess fanatics. The rain earlier that day had chased all but the last two groups. Piper walked straight toward the seven concrete chess tables situated at the northeast perimeter of the circle. I, in the meantime, took up an outpost directly behind a humpbacked gentleman who was listening intently to the harangue of a Gorgon-haired woman named (according to the outsized name tag jostling on her bosom) "Sister Althea Mungerson, Apostle to the Damned."

Shortly after Diggery reached the throng of old men and young, rich men and poor, black men and white who were clustered around the games then in progress, one of the two competitors at the central board appeared to despair of his chances and to surrender his seat to the Captain. Now, I had played four or five times myself with a few of the regulars there and was somewhat familiar with the rigid code of behavior they enforced. In that class-free gathering, worldly fortune, status and power count for naught and derelict outranks diplomat if his chess is stronger. A losing player rarely if ever cedes his place before checkmate is given, and a fresh arrival is never permitted to play ahead of the ever-present onlookers waiting their turn. The exception made that morning seemed to hinge on the technicality that Piper was not starting a new game but merely adopting the desperate position of a friend.

"...But the born-again Christian sees through such trickery and wiles. He sees these deceptions for what they are—nothing less than the works and pomps of Beelzebub himself..." With gravel-filled voice and wrenching earnestness Sister Mungerson (whose corpulent, quivering body screened me quite adequately from the chess tables a mere twenty feet or so in the distance) trumpeted her evangelical message to the scurrying passers-by. The diminutive, white haired man behind whom I stood made not a sound. In fact, save for the good sister and for her male counterpart who was working the southwest quadrant of the circle, the park was perfectly quiet. Famished pigeons pecked at the dirt and concrete for orts, squirrels darted noiselessly across the expanses of rain-slicked grass, and splendid armies of white chessmen and black marched just as silently upon one another's positions.

Each concrete playing surface was surrounded by four stationary stools which served equally well as seats or footrests. It was understood by all that the two unused stools were to be made available during a game not for kibitzers but for the combatants' *impedimenta*. Thus, when he took his place behind the black pieces, Diggery laid his briefcase on the empty stool to his left. This I was most careful to note. And yet when he rose to leave the table twenty minutes later, he swept from the stool to his right a case that was indistinguishable from the one he had brought with him and from the one he had slipped to Reginald Graves.

"...There is no refuge," Althea shrieked as Piper strode nonchalantly from the park, "nay, neither refuge nor respite in this world or the next for him who prevaricates, for him who would deceive his fellow man..."

With the irony of this sermon still echoing in my mind, I descended once more into the subterranean depths and stalked my quarry back to his lair. Just how many fellow men besides me had Diggery deceived, I asked myself over and over as we waited, one hundred feet apart, for the eastbound train to rumble into the station? And Reginald. What shady business had he gotten himself involved in? By the time we had been whooshed through the coal-black tunnels and bright, vaulted stations between uptown and the Hill, I was sick to the soul of pondering such painful matters and of slinking about the city like some scruffy Dickensian low-life. I'd had my fill of depressing discoveries for the day (or so I thought) and wanted nothing more than to plod back to my townhouse flat, transfer my cold, damp feet from boots to basin, and sleep. But alas, it was not yet to be. I was not destined to return home that morning before watching the final scene of the Captain's three-act play.

I took the stairs instead of the escalator at the Capitol south exit so as to exert fuller control over my emergence from the station. (Another pointer provided by M. Rossignol.) And fortunate it was that I did. For Diggery was waiting right there on the corner and would surely have discovered me if I'd suddenly popped up onto street level like a piece of done toast. Instead I was able to lurk quietly five steps below the head of the staircase and watch a ludicrously bewigged Sally McGonigle come prancing down First Street. Her ersatz beehive of raven-black hair had somehow been knocked askew, thus allowing a few reddish-brown locks to peek out in the region of her left ear. Judging from his sour expression, Diggery seemed to be about as impressed with the effectiveness of Sally's disguise as I was, but he hewed to the established discipline of exchanging briefcases in silence, then quickly moving along. A two-way flow of information, I mused. From House Foreign Affairs, through Diggery, to the operative in Dupont Circle; then back again, via the same conduit, to Senate Foreign Relations. Requests in one direction, replies in the other.

Once Piper was well out of sight, I climbed to the top of the stairs and watched poor, misguided Sally continue down First. It was not difficult to guess what she would do now: double back toward Constitution, stash the wig in her purse somewhere along the way, then waltz back into the committee staffroom as if she were returning from one of her half-hour coffee breaks and not, God save us, from an act of high treason.

Episode VII

In Which the Narrator is Given a Lesson in Chess...
(January 10, 1983)

What does one do with such bitter knowledge? To whom does one turn? That afternoon and night I spent brooding over the discoveries I had made and examining my unappetizing choices. Could I report three friends to the authorities on the basis of some rigamarole about an Arabian emirate and a bag-switching routine complete with disguises? Then again, could I remain silent and punch in at the mailroom as usual the next morning, as if nothing untoward were going on? Or could I take the responsibility of tipping off the suspects that their cover had been blown and approach them directly with my concerns? The answer did not come that day, nor for several days thereafter. Every restless night I spent weighing the strengths and weaknesses of those options left me more and more confused as to the proper balance to strike between loyalty and friendship on the one hand, and civic duty on the other. It was not in fact until the following Monday evening, a mere hour before the club game was due to begin, that I finally resolved to confront the architect of my moral dilemma.

"Terence!" cried Diggery, as he walked up to me in the Jefferson Lounge. The parrot sat, as ever, on his right shoulder, busily preening her green and gold feathers. "About that seven-notrump hand last week," he said cheerily. "No offense taken, I hope. Hermione asked me to extend you her heartfelt apologies. She really had no place butting in like that." His hale and hearty manner piqued me no end. Here I was agonizing over such weighty matters as treason and espionage, and he would talk of nothing but Ratchet Squeezes. "Spare me this drivel," I wanted to shout, "and prove to me you're not a spy. Prove to me that you and Reginald and Sally McGonigle are not trafficking in secrets of state." But I could not. Not out in the open like that. I had decided to stage a far more subtle confrontation.

"No offense taken," said I, meekly accepting the portion of crow I was being offered.

"Say, old boy, who are you playing with this evening? Reginald, I'll wager."

"I'm not playing with anyone tonight. I'm just not in the mood to play bridge or any other game. If you don't mind, I'll be kibitzing your game. Anyway, I'm surprised you haven't asked Reginald to be your partner by now. The two of you seem to work so well together."

"What do you mean, ducks? Why, I only just met the chap last week."

"Even so," I replied with as cryptic an undertone as I could manage, "even so." And as I slunk off to brood in an unoccupied corner of the room, I noticed that the cocky look had vanished from the Captain's face. Clearly a seed had been planted.

A full three hours passed before the moment of truth arrived. All night long I had sat, tongue-tied, staring over Diggery's left shoulder as he and Sally demolished pair after East-West pair. But when Reginald and his partner sat down to play at the seventh round I saw my chance. Not only did I now have all three suspects before me (I was Nick Charles, Simon Templar, the Falcon, rounding up all the principals for a climactic attribution of guilt), but the fact that Graves was playing with a cherubic college-age Congressional intern named Tommy Meyer—the boy's eager gaze betrayed his boundless gratitude at being permitted to play in such a high-powered game—virtually assured that our conversation would not be interrupted.

I let the first two boards pass in silence, but steeled myself for action during the bidding of the hand you see here:

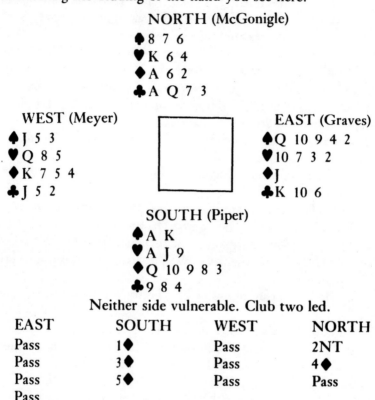

NORTH (McGonigle)
♠ 8 7 6
♥ K 6 4
♦ A 6 2
♣ A Q 7 3

WEST (Meyer)
♠ J 5 3
♥ Q 8 5
♦ K 7 5 4
♣ J 5 2

EAST (Graves)
♠ Q 10 9 4 2
♥ 10 7 3 2
♦ J
♣ K 10 6

SOUTH (Piper)
♠ A K
♥ A J 9
♦ Q 10 9 8 3
♣ 9 8 4

Neither side vulnerable. Club two led.

EAST	SOUTH	WEST	NORTH
Pass	1♦	Pass	2NT
Pass	3♦	Pass	4♦
Pass	5♦	Pass	Pass
Pass			

And a fascinating bit of bidding it was. Sally's response to Diggery's diamond opening would have been a faultless call if she had not long ago been ordered never to let the sacred word "notrump" pass her lips, save when raising such a bid made by her partner. For Diggery had determined as far back as the infamous "club thing" incident that he would do all in his power to avoid ever again sitting dummy to McGonigle's declarer. With that policy in mind, Piper now wrestled the hand into five

80

diamonds—a contract which, I could readily see, had the double disadvantage (a) of earning the South declarer who made it the same 400 points which every North declarer in the room was due to receive for bringing home a cold three notrump, and (b) of being unmakable. You see, from where I sat, both the South and West hands were an open book. What I knew and what Diggery did not was that the heart and club finesses were off and that the diamond King, although situated on the favorable side, was still immune to capture. This would be the hand on which I'd jump from the bushes, I told myself. But for the moment, I sat back and bided my time.

Meyer led out the two of clubs, a rather inhospitable choice, and Piper lapsed immediately into a three-minute meditation. When he finally emerged and called for the dummy's three I was sure he'd committed a blunder. From his vantage point the club and heart hooks were his only hope. In any case, Reginald alertly captured the trick with his ten and shifted to a spade. Once in, Piper played the trump Queen. Meyer correctly ducked, but East's Jack was pinned.

"A smother play," I commented with hidden purpose, for at last I saw my opening.

"I suppose," replied Diggery, "but I must say, this common variety of smother is—how do you Yanks put it?—a dime a dozen."

"I see. Not as rare as in the game of chess, then?"

Sally and Reginald exchanged the shadow of a glance at this oblique reference and Piper seemed to freeze. The intern kept mulling over the defensive possibilities of his own hand, as if nothing were transpiring around him.

Reginald was the first to speak up. "You should know better than to comment on a play while you're kibitzing, Terry. It's impolite—sometimes even unwise—to poke into other people's business."

"Poppycock!" said the Captain as he led the diamond ten, drawing the five from West, the six from dummy and from East a spade sluff. "And in any event his point is well taken. There is an uncommon, smashingly elegant checkmate by smother that works itself out in this manner..." Here he quickly sketched out the following diagram on the back of a spare scoresheet:

"...When the black Knight captures at Bishop seven, the enemy King is suffocated by the very three of his subjects whose charge it has been to protect him." Diggery casually cashed the spade King now, having fully regained his composure.

"You haven't by any chance seen such a trap sprung lately, have you?" I pressed on. "Last Tuesday morning, say?"

"Excuse me," Sally interjected. "I'm not feeling too well. Would you mind turning my cards, Reginald, while I run off to the powder room?" Graves agreed, although he looked as peaked as she did. Piper, on the other hand, did not so much as blink. And if he did not answer my question directly, at least he stuck to the subject at hand.

"You know, Terence," he began, in a characteristic resort to verbal subterfuge, "there are more parellels than you might think between the games of chess and bridge. Take the three principal resources in chess, for example: time, position and material. They happen to be the most lethal arrows in the bridge master's quiver as well."

"Are they really?" I would indulge him for a moment. He was obviously running scared.

"Yes, yes. Here, let me try to demonstrate with this very deal. I take it we all realize by now that every other North/South pair in this room will make three notrump by dint of sheer material since South, once he drives out the diamond King, holds nine master

82

cards. But in five diamonds, I do not have the luxury of relying on outright force. No, I must fall back on a careful orchestration of tempo and position. I begin with the standard chess practice of shifting one's attack from the less promising to the more promising side of the board." And he tabled the Jack of hearts. The poor intern had no option but to cover, North's King taking the trick. The heart four was called for next and Piper completed the backward finesse by inserting his nine when Reginald played low. The Ace of hearts then eliminated that suit from West's hand. "Bear in mind," Diggery cautioned, "that the desperate measures I have adopted here are predicated on the premise that if either one of the rounded-suit finesses is on, a declarer in diamonds will never be able to match the score of a declarer in notrump. And so my perverse line of play is actually forced. If I am to prevail, East must hold the club King and the ten—but not the Queen—of hearts." He now led straight to his club Ace, spurning the finesse for a second time. When he followed up with a spade ruff, he voided the intern of that suit as well. The position was now:

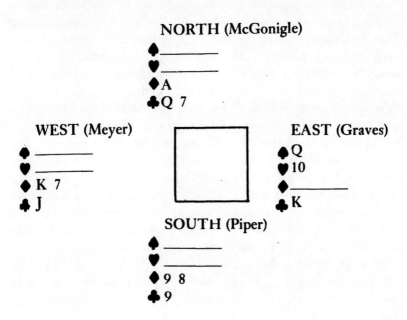

NORTH (McGonigle)
♠ —————
♥ —————
♦ A
♣ Q 7

WEST (Meyer)
♠ —————
♥ —————
♦ K 7
♣ J

EAST (Graves)
♠ Q
♥ 10
♦ —————
♣ K

SOUTH (Piper)
♠ —————
♥ —————
♦ 9 8
♣ 9

83

The foresight behind the Captain's ducking in dummy at trick one was finally revealed, for when he now led the club nine at the crucial eleventh trick, East, with his King, was compelled to take the lead, while poor Meyer was stripped of yet another suit.

"Checkmate!" announced Piper, triumphantly dropping his 9-8 of diamonds to the table. "Thanks to a judicious management of position and timing, we may yet earn an average score on this board."

Reginald, the intern and I silently contemplated that freak ending. In time, we reached the inescapable conclusion that whether East now chose to lead his spade or his heart, West's cherished trump King—which for so long had appeared to be as snugly protected as the monarch in the Captain's chess diagram—was doomed to strangulation. "Now *there*," declared Diggery, "is a smother play worthy of the name."

I must admit that the Captain's Fabian tactic succeeded admirably. For from the moment that hand was completed until the hour when the gameroom was populated by no more than a handful of dawdlers loitering around the scoretable and trading tales of unreciprocated brilliance, I sequestered myself with a deck of cards in an anteroom of the lounge and searched in vain for a way to resuscitate that lifeless King of trumps. Yet I could find no opening lead (not even the Jack of clubs will do) nor any subsequent shift by East that would have altered his Highness's grisly fate. Two full hours I spent there, oblivious to the real world and to the urgency of the night's forgotten mission. But when midnight struck and the uniformed Capitol guard came by to lock up, I finally returned to my senses. I ran through the halls of the Old Senate Office Building and out onto Constitution Avenue, intent on hunting Diggery down and wrangling the truth from him once and for all. This time I would put the question to him face to face. This time I would brook no diversions.

My search ended the moment it began. No sooner did I charge out into the frosty night air than I spotted the three of them huddled about a wrought-iron bench in the northeast quadrant of the ellipse, their figures silhouetted against the floodlit facade of the Capitol itself. I quickly crossed Constitution and entered the oak-filled sward that separates the Capitol from the Library of Congress and the Supreme Court. While I did not purposely avail myself of the convenient cover of darkness to eavesdrop, it proved impossible not to overhear snatches of the conspirators' conversation which wafted my way on the stiff evening breeze. Innocent bridge phrases like "the five of spades" and "the last hand," and the not so innocent espionage term, "microdot."

I'd read my Ludlum and my Le Carré. I'd browsed through the National Archives collection of miniaturized Nazi intelligence messages intercepted by the Allies during World War II. I knew what a microdot was.

"So!" I exclaimed, once I was ten paces or so from where they stood. The three of them started and turned toward me with horrified expressions. "Caught you in the act, didn't I?" I no longer even gave them the benefit of the doubt.

"*Shhhhh!*" came Sally's reply, following a moment of confused silence. "Keep it down, will you? They could be watching us this very minute."

"Don't tell me to *shhhh*, you little Quisling. What makes you think I'd care if 'they' were? What makes you think I won't leave here right now and put a well-deserved end to this sleazy operation the three of you and God knows how many others are running?"

"Because," said Diggery, "we refuse to believe that you are a traitor to your country." Such a blaze of authority burned in his eyes as he delivered himself of this bizarre statement that I found myself temporarily incapable of responding to, or even comprehending, the implications of its topsy-turvy logic. "Can you swear to us," he went on, "that you are not one of them?"

"'Them'? Just who do you mean by 'them'?"

"There isn't a chance in the world," Reginald said in my defense. "I've known him for almost a year now. Believe me, he's as straight as they come."

"What in the world are you..."

"Do you have any idea," Piper interrupted me, "of what you've stumbled onto?"

"I...I'm not sure..."

"You don't, do you? No idea whatsoever."

"Well, no. But...but I certainly intend to..."

"And yet you take it upon yourself to blurt out information of the most sensitive nature while sitting in the middle of a room full of people."

"But it wasn't as if I screamed it out," I pleaded, not at all sure of the exact moment when I'd been maneuvered into a defensive position. "I mean, all I did was hint at what I knew. Look, I'm sure that intern Reginald was playing with didn't..."

"All right, all right, forget about it," Diggery snapped in a manner suggesting to all present that the usefulness of the previous topic of conversation had been thoroughly exhausted. "You are looking at an undercover agent of Interpol," he said, indicating himself, "and at two American citizens authorized by your government's National Security Agency to cooperate with me and my cadre of co-agents on a mission of the direst import." Here he handed me credentials which bore a photograph that in some respects resembled his face as I saw it now and in others as I had seen it, in disguised form, the previous Tuesday morning, but that was in turn as different from those two visages as it was similar.

The embarrassment I felt then was surpassed only by an acute sense of relief that my friends were innocent. That even if they were spies, they were not traitors. "I...I had no idea that..."

"For two and one half years now, ever since the 1980 Bridge Olympiad in Sao Paolo, Brazil, to be exact, the three of us and our support personnel have been implementing a long-range plan designed to destroy a nefarious espionage ring which, for almost a decade, has been using the forum of national and international bridge tournaments as a front for their activities, and whose goals and objectives are categorically opposed to those shared by all law-respecting societies."

"Then...then what you told me about coming to America for the Bicentennial celebration..."

"Oh, Lordy," moaned Sally with a heavenward roll of the eyes. "Are you telling me he actually used that hokey story

86

about...Whoops! Sorry, Terry."

"But why me?" I asked, my mortification mounting with each fresh revelation. "Was it by pure accident that Diggery and I turned out to be partners those first two weeks?"

"It was no accident," Reginald answered. "I cleared you for what we call 'unaware participation' as far back as last September. You were Piper's safe ticket into the club until Sally completed her training in Europe and arrived back on the scene. Frankly, we'd hoped you'd quietly..."

"Bug off?"

"...Right, but it didn't work out that way. We didn't count on your, well, your persistence."

"By the way," said Piper sharply, "what exactly did you hear as you approached us just now?"

"Nothing," I answered. "Just...just some bridge talk about the last hand in tonight's game."

"What else?" he insisted.

"Nothing. Nothing else." I decided, whether out of fear or residual skepticism, to conceal the part about the microdot. To hold it back, just in case, against the time when I might want to play it as a trump card. "I have some questions myself, you know. Why are you using the Congressional Club? And what was in those briefcases you kept passing back and forth last Tuesday morning? And what happens to me now?" Just as I was beginning to regain my confidence, I noticed that Piper and Graves were scarcely listening to me. They seemed instead to be concentrating on a black Mercedes-Benz which cruised nearby us, then slowed to a stop at the corner of Delaware and Constitution. It was difficult to distinguish very much in the faint night light at that distance, but there appeared to be a rather short man sitting behind the driver's wheel and no one beside him or in the back seat. He doused his lights but remained in the car.

Diggery spoke quickly now, his eyes never veering from the auto. "The answer to your last question is that you are now one of us. You know too much to be running about on the loose. Your other question will be answered as the mission proceeds, and as the sense of discretion you display does or does not warrant. We

87

will not meet again for five days. On Saturday evening next, at precisely seven-thirty, we will convene in my flat to begin our sessions on strategy and tactics preparatory to the start of the competition early next month." The Captain allowed himself a quick smile, clapped me on the shoulder and said, "Welcome aboard, Kane," before striding off toward Independence Avenue, in the opposite direction of the parked Mercedes. The others began to leave too, Reginald hurrying toward the bus stop at the south side of the ellipse and Sally angling across the grass toward the residential section of Capitol Hill.

"Wait!" I called out to anyone who would listen. "What competition?"

"You don't know?" I heard Sally call back through the darkness. "The Knockouts, silly. The Grand National Team Knockouts." And the last sound I heard was her childlike giggle which, by its very inappropriateness, had the effect not of diminishing but of augmenting my sense of apprehension.

Episode VIII

In Which the Piper Quartet Is Formed...
                                          (January 15, 1983)

"Come in, Terence, come in," said Diggery, who, when he met me at the door of his Bradley Arms apartment, wore a hunter-green smoking jacket, a silken scarf of eggshell white and a truly embracing smile. My spirits were soaring high. Here I was entering the supersecret planning session of a team of crack espionage agents. I felt I'd watched enough *Mission Impossible* reruns to know in general terms the kinds of things I would be told that night. Piper, as Jim Phelps, would give an overview of the assignment, complete with surveillance film clips and stills of the culprits we were up against. Reginald would next explain how his specialty—something akin to Barney's devilish electronic skill, say—fit into the overall plan. Then Sally would be impressed with the necessity of her participating in the type of sexual scenario which Barbara Bain's Cinnamon always brought off with such teasing, virginal flair. It remained to determine what they had in mind for me. Peter Lupus's herculean feats of strength? Facial-vocal deception à la Martin Landau, the master of disguises? Or perhaps some other role—one a bit more suited to my own peculiar talents.

I would no doubt be issued a code name. My position at the Congressional mailroom would from here on in be thought of not as my job but as my cover. Tax-free compensation would be piped to me by some clandestine means. The mystery of the microdot would be explained. All of this was exciting enough, but I was looking forward too to seeing my first "safe-house"—one of those ultra-secure environments allegedly maintained by the CIA (or "the Company," as I had privately resolved to refer to my new colleagues) in hundreds of locations throughout the country. The Captain's would, of course, be spectacular; opulent to the point of decadence. *Le dernier mot* in hideaways.

I would now exhort you, dear reader, to erase from your mind, as I was forced to do, any image of grandeur you may have conjured up in an effort to envision those living quarters. For Diggery's safe-house, alas, was a dump.

"Make yourself comfortable," Piper said as he showed me past a windowless, formica-rife kitchen and a bedroom that contained no more than a glorified cot, a dressing table, a ratty chest of drawers and an antique pine wardrobe partially stripped of its stain and varnish and encrusted with a chocolate-brown patina of paint. The room we entered was larger than the bedroom but just as unsavory in appearance. There were no paintings, no carpets, no knick-knack-filled étagères, no lamps, no sofa, no hassocks, no easy chairs of any kind. Just a three-legged pearwood stand supporting a moribund African violet, four straightbacked chairs and a fold-up table almost but not quite centered below the tackiest of metal lighting fixtures. And, dominating one half of the room, an enormous ceiling-mounted cage, behind the bamboo bars of which Hermione—the erstwhile bane of my existence—gently rocked to and fro on a perch.

"Why don't you take a seat at the table, Terence, and I'll bring you something to drink," Diggery suggested. But just as I was about to place my order (two fingers of Tanqueray, neat) he inquired as to whether I preferred coffee or tea.

"Oh, uh, tea, I guess. Unless you've got a drop or two of..."

"I'm afraid there'll be none of that tonight, old chap."

"I understand. Serious business, eh?"

"Now there's the attitude we're looking for. You know, there are quite a number of self-described professionals around who cling to the delusion that bridge is a game. It's no wonder they never make it to the top."

"No, I meant..."

"Excuse me." The bell had rung. When Piper returned to the living room he had Graves and McGonigle in tow. As the two of them said hello, took seats at the table and ordered a coffee and a tea, I scrutinized their faces for any traces of the anxiety I myself was feeling; any intimation that the knowledge the three of us now shared (we who for the better part of a year had walked through the paces of a false, albeit necessarily false, relationship) was a source of at least minor embarrassment. But I detected no such indications. There sat Reginald to my left, just as quiet and correct, just as stolidly uncommunicative as ever. And there to my right sat Sally, beaming that hopelessly seraphic smile of hers. A smile that always had been, and would forever remain, bereft of the slightest trace of irony. A smile so open, so vulnerable, that I wondered whether she had consciously dissimulated during the long months of her Congressional Club and Senate Foreign Relations Committee performances, or if her overwhelming naiveté was so natural and so ingrained a character trait that she had never had to bother to put it on in the morning and take it off at night like an article of clothing. There was a time, admittedly, when I had not known what was going on; but now I did. And my words, my actions, my demeanor would naturally reflect that difference. Not so, I'm afraid, with Sally. To her it was all the same. The way she looked at this moment, seated and smiling in this stark, dingy room, was no different from the way she looked when I first met her, seated and smiling in the splendor of the Jefferson Lounge: like an exquisite porcelain vase. Too visually prepossessing not to be left out in full view, but far too fragile to serve any practical purpose.

"Well, did y'all believe how cold it was today?" Sally asked as we waited for Diggery to bring in the refreshments. The woman recognized no rival in the art of making small talk.

"Yes, yes," replied Graves. "It was cold all right...real cold."

"Yep. You know, we had days like this one all winter long back when I was a girl in Enid, Oklahoma. Not as damp, maybe, but just as cold. Shoot, I can remember one day in particular when..." Incredibly, she began spinning out a protracted tale about her family's clapboard farmhouse, three brown heifers, a ramshackle barn and a winter storm in 1966—a tale that could not possibly have been more foreign in subject or tone to the evening's real agenda. How could she do this? I recall asking myself. How could she trivialize our high purpose so blatantly? How could she babble on about farms and livestock when we had such serious matters to discuss?

For a good five minutes that story dragged on, until Sally's voice finally rose in volume as she homed in on her punch line: "...So my papa says, (and here she adopted a husky male tone) 'You know, I was just out back and it's colder out there'n the south side of a...'"

"Well, here we are," announced Diggery as he walked into the room carrying a trayful of teacups and a squat ceramic pot that emitted the dark, musty fragrance of Keemun. For Reginald there was a steaming mug of coffee. "Let's begin, shall we?"

"Actually," I said, half out of common courtesy and half out of some compulsion to hear the last few words of that inane anecdote, "Sally was about to finish a..."

"Oh, it wasn't important," she cut in.

"Well, I realize that but, after all, you were just on the verge of..."

"No," she insisted. "Now that we're all here, I think we should get right down to business."

"I agree," said Reginald emphatically.

"I should say," Diggery chimed in. All three of them were glaring at me as if I had been the one who'd first brought up the story about the cold day in Oklahoma.

"Okay, okay. Look, it suits me fine. On to the strategy and tactics."

"A capital idea," said Piper. "Shall we start with the nature of trump promotion?" He pulled a stiff new deck of cards from the pocket of his smoking jacket and began sorting it briskly into suits.

92

"Wait, hold on a minute," I protested. "I thought we were here to prepare ourselves for our assignment."

"We are," said Reginald. "But who's better qualified to train us than the Captain? He's easily the best player of the four of us, isn't he?"

"Well, of course he is."

"Look, old boy," said Diggery, "if you'd rather take over..."

"No, that's not what I mean. I don't want to take over. It's just that I thought...well, I expected to learn more about...you know..."

"Ah, about defense and bidding as opposed to the play of the hand? Well, here's my theory on that. I believe bidding and defense are virtually unteachable skills which, unlike declarer play, depend far more on judgment and intuition than on straightforward technique."

"No, no. I was hoping to get more basic information about who we are, what we're about, the kind of characters we'll be up against, where we expect to be a month from now, six months from now, whatever." And then one by one, whether out of sheer obtuseness or a conspiracy of selective silence, the three of them began spouting information calculated to satisfy my fathomless curiosity only at the shallowest levels and to keep submerged in a sea of darkness the spy dope I was so eager to hear.

"'Who we are,'" offered Diggery, "is a team called the Piper Quartet, one of more than nine thousand four- to six-member squads slated to compete in this year's Grand National Knockout tournament. 'What we're about' is winning a months-long competition that starts at the American Contract Bridge League district level—where scores of teams such as ours battle it out in local knockout, double-knockout, Swiss or round-robin matches—then moves on to division-level championships held in major cities throughout the country. Following that, there are the zonal play-offs, from which eight finalists emerge, then the national championships in San Francisco this summer, where a single winner will be determined. And the sobering truth of the matter is, if we do not garner a place in that final session, we will have failed altogether in our mission."

"But I still don't have a very clear idea as to..."

"Oh, right," said Reginald, "as to 'the kind of characters we'll be up against.' Wasn't that the third item in your complaint? Well, who our opponents are will naturally depend on what happens in matches other than our own, since teams will constantly be either advancing or dropping out. I can tell you, though, that we're scheduled to face our first opponents a week from next Friday. Some team representing the Library of Congress. If we win that, we'll play..."

"You mean *when* we win that," Sally corrected.

"...Yes, *when* we win that, we'll play the winner of a match pitting the Pentagon Pummelers against the IRS Taxonomists. Diggery's already explained our long-range projections. What I've just told you should answer your question about where we'll be a month from now."

"Yes, but..."

"So I guess you can see," said Sally, coming in right on cue, "why these thirteen bridge lessons the Captain's agreed to give us are so darned impor——"

"Thirteen lessons!"

"Why, yes," said Piper. "A three-hour session per night, every night, until the day of our first match. Unless, of course, that would work an undue hardship on you from the point of view of scheduling. I realize this is short notice indeed."

"No, no, that's not it. I just don't understand why players of our caliber" (how expansive of me, I remember thinking, to include Sally within the scope of that possessive pronoun) "should have to undergo thirty-nine hours of instruction on the finer points of declarer play."

"Oh, we won't be spending very much time on the finer points," Diggery replied. "The brunt of my lectures, in point of fact, will bear on the fundamentals. *Tabula rasa* is the only effective way to begin, really. How, after all, can one be expected to execute a Double Grand Coup in the crucible of expert competition if one has not first mastered the humble art of finessing?"

"Finessing? Do you mean to tell me you're going to teach us about finessing? God, I learned almost everything there is to know about finishing the first day I sat down to play. The rest I picked up in Richard Frey's *How to Win at Contract Bridge in Ten Easy Lessons.*"

"Well, then perhaps you've spared me a great deal of effort. But just to be sure, let's see what you absorbed, shall we?" Piper gave his deck a brisk shuffle, dealt out the hand I present here and asked me, as his partner, to begin the bidding:

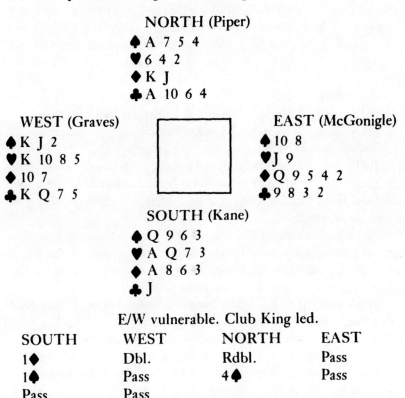

NORTH (Piper)
♠ A 7 5 4
♥ 6 4 2
♦ K J
♣ A 10 6 4

WEST (Graves)
♠ K J 2
♥ K 10 8 5
♦ 10 7
♣ K Q 7 5

EAST (McGonigle)
♠ 10 8
♥ J 9
♦ Q 9 5 4 2
♣ 9 8 3 2

SOUTH (Kane)
♠ Q 9 6 3
♥ A Q 7 3
♦ A 8 6 3
♣ J

E/W vulnerable. Club King led.

SOUTH	WEST	NORTH	EAST
1♦	Dbl.	Rdbl.	Pass
1♠	Pass	4♠	Pass
Pass	Pass		

"Anyone vulnerable?" I asked, once again submitting to the sweet tyranny of a handful of cards.

"That depends. Do you feel vulnerable?"

"Not really," I answered, provoked by his baiting tone. How well he knew, has always known, how to manipulate my emotions. It took no more than those thirteen cards to make me relegate our mission to the back of my mind. I was suffering from an attack of bridge fever.

"Very well, then. Let us assume that Reginald and Miss Sally are vulnerable but that we are not."

I opened a diamond, Graves doubled, Piper redoubled and Sally passed. I then bid a spade, which Diggery promptly raised to game. Reginald led out the King of clubs as Piper rose from his seat and took a position behind me, leaving me to turn dummy's cards. If he had limited himself to merely observing I might not have minded, but the first thing he did was to lean forward and whisper, "In the future, I suggest you pass your partner's strong redoubles and see where the opposition runs. Also, do remember to bid your four-card suits *up* the line when responding. This hand should actually have been played from my side."

"Do you mind?" I asked aloud. "I'm trying to concentrate."

"But of course. Please excuse the interruption." Yet it was hardly his last. Once I had devised a plan of attack and reached for the club Ace, he said: "Pardon me, Terence, but it might prove instructive for us all if you explained what you think you need to make this contract."

"Oh, I guess things will work out if I bring in a couple of onside finesses and luck into a break in the trump suit," I answered sarcastically, as little impressed with my chances of making the game as I was with Piper's decision to bid it.

"A subtle analysis," said Diggery. "You know, I may well have underestimated your acumen, at that."

Somewhat bolstered by this admission, I went about the business of playing out the hand. I captured the King of clubs in dummy and played a trump down to my Queen, losing to Reginald's King. He continued with the two of spades, dummy's Ace gathering Sally's ten and my three. That left the master Jack outstanding.

Even though the hoped-for break in trumps had not materialized, all was not lost. To cash the Ace-King of diamonds now and play for two ruffs would be to accept at least a one-trick defeat, I reasoned, for even if the heart finesse worked, I would still lose the two long hearts. But if the spade Jack, heart King and diamond Queen sat favorably, and if the distribution of the two red suits turned out to be friendly as well, I would still prevail. Here, in fact, is the fantasy hand I envisioned:

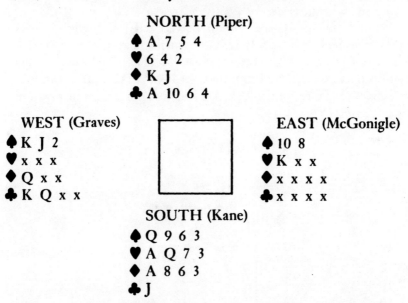

NORTH (Piper)
♠ A 7 5 4
♥ 6 4 2
♦ K J
♣ A 10 6 4

WEST (Graves)
♠ K J 2
♥ x x x
♦ Q x x
♣ K Q x x

EAST (McGonigle)
♠ 10 8
♥ K x x
♦ x x x x
♣ x x x x

SOUTH (Kane)
♠ Q 9 6 3
♥ A Q 7 3
♦ A 8 6 3
♣ J

Seeing no reason not to bank on this hypothetical layout, I ruffed a club at trick four and announced my intentions to Piper and the others. "I will now finesse the diamond Jack," I said, "in the hope of finding the Queen onside. I will then cash the diamond King, take the heart finesse, follow up with the Ace of that suit, pitch dummy's third and last heart on the Ace of diamonds and cross-ruff till the cows come home. In the end I'll score the trump seven, *en passant*, for an overtrick."

Braced by the sheer elegance of this conception, I led confidently to the diamond Jack. It lost, and that was that.

At first I felt as foolish as Rabelais's King Picrochole who, surrounded by war ministers in the safety of his strategy room, won an abstract campaign by parlaying paper skirmishes at his nearest frontiers into glorious victories throughout the farthest reaches of his enemies' realms, but whose forces were obliterated the moment they set foot on the soil of an actual battlefield. Yet as

97

I thought the matter over, what was there to be ashamed of? The four-spade contract was simply not there. Diggery had overbid. Besides, hadn't he himself agreed that declarer would have to bring in two finesses?

While I thus spent my energy in private self-exculpation, things went from bad to dreadful. Sally returned a heart at the sixth trick and my Queen quickly bit the dust. Next Reginald cashed his trump Jack and reverted to hearts. I took my Ace but found that my diamonds were now blocked. Here was the gruesome position at trick nine:

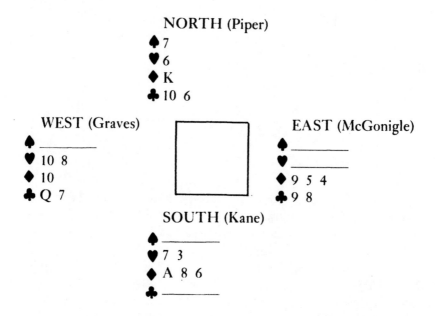

NORTH (Piper)
♠ 7
♥ 6
♦ K
♣ 10 6

WEST (Graves)
♠ ———
♥ 10 8
♦ 10
♣ Q 7

EAST (McGonigle)
♠ ———
♥ ———
♦ 9 5 4
♣ 9 8

SOUTH (Kane)
♠ ———
♥ 7 3
♦ A 8 6
♣ ———

When I played to my diamond King in dummy and surrendered a heart, Reginald still refrained from taking his club Queen. Instead he stuck me back in the North hand again by persevering with hearts and forcing a ruff. At the twelfth trick I had to lead from the 10-6 of clubs into his Q-7 as my diamond Ace languished in the closed hand.

"Down four," pronounced the Captain. "They seem to have taken one more trick than you did."

"Well, what did you expect?" I fumed. "Both finesses were off, the trump King was on the wrong side and neither red suit broke evenly. Remember, you agreed with my plan of attack, and so would've run into the same rotten luck."

"I beg to differ, old boy. In the first place, you will recall that the word I used in characterizing your initial analysis was 'subtle', not 'accurate'. Admittedly it is reasonable—if unnecessary—to take two finesses here, but even then not in the heart and diamond suits."

"Where then?"

"In spades, naturally. And furthermore, I had no idea you intended to ignore the one suit that is the key to this problem's solution."

"Clubs, I suppose?"

"Clubs indeed."

"Prove it," I challenged, vacating my chair. Surely Piper was talking through his hat. I was willing to concede that the hand might go down only two or three tricks with some convoluted line, but was convinced that even prior knowledge of the entire layout would not suffice to bring the contract in safely.

"You are saying to yourself," Diggery began, "that I will contrive a double-dummy offense in an attempt to make the hand. But I invite you to stop me the moment you feel my play is based on anything but keen observation, commonsense deduction and a thorough understanding of the innate strengths and weaknesses of that most popular and least understood of bridge maneuvers: the finesse."

"Agreed," said I, and the fat was in the fire.

"To begin with," Diggery began, addressing his comments to the entire class, "Terence committed numbers two and six of what I call 'The Seven Deadly Sins of Declarer Play at Bridge.' We will examine all seven and their most common manifestations over the course of this lecture series, but the particular transgressions that apply in this case are: Failure to Draw from the Bidding and Defense Any Clues That Might Aid in the Play of the Hand, and Failure to Determine Which Finesses Can Safely Be Taken and Which Finesses Can Safely Be Avoided."

99

"Sounds pretty serious," said McGonigle.

"Quite. As you will see, Miss Sally, each offense cost our woebegone declarer an average of two tricks. But such are the wages of sin. Now, once Reginald leads the King of clubs, Terence must say to himself, 'There sits a man who holds the Queen as well'..."

"Fat lot of good that's going to do me when the South hand has nothing to finesse with."

"There you go again, lunging at finesses. Suffice it to say that the presence of the club Queen in West's hand will have definite implications for the play of your heart suit. But that information is best stored for the time being, as the first task before you is the management of your trumps. You can infer two things from Reginald's vulnerable, second-seat double. What are they?"

"Well, that he's got an opening hand..."

"And?"

"And presumably enough length in each of the majors to support a bid by his partner in either suit."

"Good show. It's clear you've done your reading. My goal, you see, is to make the book knowledge you've stockpiled over the years available to you on a hand-to-hand basis. Now to continue. Given West's call, I place him with at least three spades and almost surely all three missing Kings. Thus it makes little sense to squander the spade Queen at trick two, now doesn't it? You see, the only 'break' I'm looking for in the trump suit is that West hold three rather than four spades and that one of them be the deuce."

"The deuce?" asked Reginald. He too seemed to be turning into a doubting Thomas on this one.

"The deuce. Is that too much to ask? Now, if West should turn up with four trumps, the hand is unlikely to make in any case and I will have to resort, as Terence did, to a flurry of desperate finesses in the side suits. But my initial attack on spades will be based on the assumption that Reginald was dealt the K-J-2, the K-10-2 or the K-8-2. A generous range of possibilities, you will have to admit. And so, at trick one I take my club Ace in dummy and lead a low trump." Sally played the eight and Diggery the nine.

100

Reginald won the trick with his Jack. "There you have my first finesse," said Piper. "The second will presently be forthcoming."

When Reginald shifted to a diamond, I waited for the Captain to play the Jack, but he did not. "Presently," he repeated as he took his King, "presently." He then ruffed a club in the closed hand and tabled the Queen of trumps, thereby completing a vicious double finesse I suddenly remembered having read about in the January 1975 issue of the *American Contract Bridge League Bulletin*.

"Gabriel Chagas!" I cried out as Reginald and Sally mourned the apparent demise of their trump trick. (Although, as it developed, the spade King would later rise from the dead.) "The Bols tip-of-the-month in the 'Masterpointers' section. A two-stage stratagem which Chagas called the 'intra-finesse.' Why didn't I remember it when I was playing the hand?"

"Think back once again to the Second Deadly Sin," Piper counseled. "Had you worked it out that the King was offside, this elegant, if superfluous, gambit might well have occurred to you."

"Hold it. What do you mean by 'superfluous'?"

"Simply that even when managing the trumps the way you did, declarer should not fail to make four spades. Now, do you want Reginald to cover the Queen or not? Either way Miss Sally's ten is snuffed out."

"Let him keep the King," I said.

"Very well. Oh, by the way, the running of the trump Queen represents the second and final finesse I plan to take. I cash my diamond Ace at trick six, then ruff a diamond in dummy..." (It would have done Reginald no good whatsoever to trump in here, so he sluffed a heart.) "... Next I ruff a club in hand and trump my last diamond with dummy's Ace. This leaves me two tricks shy of making my bid. I suggest we all reveal our last four cards at this point so that Terence can see how the contract comes home." Here was the situation:

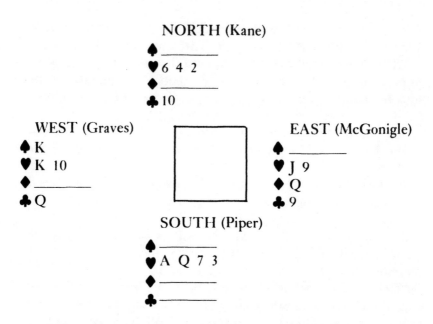

NORTH (Kane)
♠ _____
♥ 6 4 2
♦ _____
♣ 10

WEST (Graves)
♠ K
♥ K 10
♦ _____
♣ Q

EAST (McGonigle)
♠ _____
♥ J 9
♦ Q
♣ 9

SOUTH (Piper)
♠ _____
♥ A Q 7 3
♦ _____
♣ _____

"Of course!" cried Reginald. "You force me into the lead by playing the ten of clubs from dummy, at last making use of the inference you drew at trick one when my King promised the Queen."

"Just so."

"I get my trump King, but then..."

"Then you get to take one crucial finesse after all," I complained somewhat bad-naturedly to Diggery.

"Not so," he objected. "I can hardly be blamed if my opponents insist on leading away from their honors, can I?" And at this point Hermione circled the confines of her bamboo domain and broke the quarter hour of silence she had until then maintained by letting out three squawks of unrestrained delight. Once those shrieks had put my objection into proper perspective, Diggery resumed his lecture. "You see, class, Terence underutilized all three of his most precious resources: the nine of spades, the ten of clubs and his imagination. Tonight's session and those that follow—if I may be permitted to pick up at the point where I was interrupted—will train you to spot the clues so subtly woven into the fabric of every hand..."

That is exactly, and exclusively, what he did. Set aside for a time were the larger concerns—all questions of enemy agents and back-up personnel and code names and microdots—while our bridge cover was systematically perfected. For thirteen nights the Captain piloted Reginald, Sally and me through the myriad variables that complicate the play of the hand. The conclusions to be drawn from bids, from the absence of bids, from leads, from discards. The Seven Deadly Sins and how not to commit them. The rich veins of logic and circumspection that lie beneath the surface of the enlightened declarer's every decision. He dealt too with the mechanics of team play in which Reginald and I would compete as North/South, let us say, against two players of the opposition team while Diggery and Sally, sitting East/West at another table, played the same deals. Here he concentrated on the changes in strategy necessitated by the difference between the matchpoint scoring methods we were used to employing and the International Match Point (IMP) tally system we would encounter in the Knockouts. I would not go so far as to claim that the Captain transformed the three of us into bridge mavens of the highest order, but there was certainly a vast improvement in each player's grasp of the game's fundamentals. And, what is infinitely more important, it was during the last of those thirteen sessions, on the very eve, in fact, of our tournament debut, that the dissonant personalities of a motley team of four magically blended into the sweet, mellifluous harmony for which the Piper Quartet has since become renowned.

103

Episode IX

In Which the Captain Conducts a Round of Musical Chairs...

(January 28, 1983)

No one who gazes upon the fluted columns and hand-hewn pediments of the Library of Congress facade, or walks the length of that building's marbled halls, or scans the sun-filled void of its 160-foot-high rotunda is ever left unaffected. Hundreds of tourists marvel daily at the Carraran splendor of the walls and great staircase. They gawk at the magnificent Bible of Mainz and at the stately Gutenberg, enshrined in their glass-and-varnished-wood exhibit cases. They wonder at the stylized grace of the murals and the intricate construction of the seven vaulted ceilings, each one covered with tens of thousands of variously pigmented tiles. That Italianate structure is arguably the capital's most elegant environment. And so when Reginald informed me that we would be the guests of the Library of Congress Bibliophiles for our first Grand National match, I looked forward to a tasteful experience.

I discovered on the day of the game, however, that the Library of the tourists and casual readers is not the Library of the building's professionals—a population divided more or less equally between those federal employees who file, stamp, catalog, shelve, repair, restore, retrieve and otherwise process the 18 million-odd titles that are housed in the subterranean stacks, and the wizened old men who scurry to the choicest carrels each morning at 8:30 and conduct the most arcane research imaginable until the six bronze doors close for the night. In the eyes of every member of those two factions, the marble and murals and mosaics of the Library had long ago lost their allure and were now no more than the trappings of an all too familiar work place. There is in fact only one room in the entire six-story complex that holds sufficient cachet to coax those professionals, for an average stay of two-and one half hours per day, from their official or unofficial posts. That semi-secret chamber, located in the building's windowless depths and not even listed in the public directory, turned out to be the site of the Quartet's maiden match. And as Diggery, Sally, Reginald and I discovered upon walking through its doors at twelve noon on the last Friday of January, that room was the Library of Congress canteen.

There one searched in vain for pigmented tiles or vaulted ceilings and found instead a hodge-podge of neon, plastic and linoleum reminiscent of a hall leased by the Veterans of Foreign Wars. The noise and smoke levels, and the size of the crowd that gathered there, greatly supported the comparison. But while the VFW brethren usually keep a worthwhile pretext on hand to justify their beery shindigs—some fund-raising drive or sponsorship project which binds them all in the pursuit of a commonly shared objective—the two hundred patrons of the Library snack bar sat in discreet clusters of two to six individuals and indulged in every card game from canasta to bid whist, every board game from chess to Sorry, every manner of puzzle from jigsaws to mazes to jumbles to double acrostics. Squadrons of war gamers huddled red-eyed over Panzerblitz boards, while computer-game enthusiasts shrieked with glee every time their zapper sounded and yet another enemy battleship burbled to the depths of some abstract electronic ocean. Password and Botticelli clues rang out over the throng and merged with disembodied letters of the alphabet rising from spirited G-H-O-S-T games. The sole unifying element in this Babel of competitive interraction was that just about every desk clerk, typist, cataloguer or researcher was eating some make-believe food or drinking some chemical brew purchased at the canteen's battery of vending machines, and puffing feverishly on a cigarette or cigar. You may be assured that the aromas wafting from that room were rank and malodorous in the extreme.

We had expected to be met at the door by our opponents but no one came forward or offered us a seat. No one even looked up during the whole first quarter hour that we stood there leaning against the wall and wondering how bridge or any other game requiring intense concentration could possibly be played amid such relentless cacophony. But at precisely 12:15, a calm came over that congregation—a calm soon shattered by a lusty burst of cheering which lasted the eternity it seemed to take a newly arrived foursome of white-haired, pipe-toting elders to insinuate their way through the multitude. Once they had struggled to the very center of the room, they seated themselves at a table marked "Reserved for the Bibliophiles."

At first the men seemed oblivious to the crowd, each one laboriously cramming a plug of tobacco into the barrel of his pipe and lighting up. But this chore completed, they smiled and nodded to the audience, their heads bobbing slowly up and down like the noggins of a clutch of somber puppets. At the same time there shone a fiery alertness in each man's pupils which belied this image and put at least three of us on our guard.

"Glory, aren't they darling?" Sally whispered, shaking her head from side to side. "Shoot, there're two of them there, at least, who remind me of my daddy. Now how're you supposed to try and whip someone who reminds you of your daddy?"

In the silence that followed the initial uproar, all four of the Bibliophiles turned to the side of the room where we were standing and motioned us to approach their table. As we walked toward them and prepared to introduce ourselves I noticed that despite their remarkably similar appearance and despite the fact that they seemed always to act more or less in unison, they did not give the impression of redundancy so much as cohesion. It was as if these men who had studied together for so many years and eaten

106

together for so many meals and played so many hundreds of hours of cards during countless tea breaks and lunches now walked and smoked and nodded and waved (and, it was my fear, played bridge) as if they were four component parts of a single organism.

"You must be the members of the Piper Quartet," one of the gentlemen opened with a smile. Then, one after the other, each of his teammates offered a welcoming comment in a frail, wheezy voice. "That's a very catchy name for a team," the first man continued. "Ours is the Bibliophiles."

"That's a fine name for a team too, don't you think?" asked one of the others.

Then the shortest of the four, who wore a crumpled brown bow tie, said in Sally McGonigle's direction, "I think my colleagues and I are in for a charming afternoon no matter which way this match of ours goes."

"Oh, aren't you the sweetest little thing," gushed Sally. Then, turning toward Reginald, Piper and me: "Tell me they're not just the cuddliest little things you ever met!" Of course what I wanted to tell her was just that, lest she swallow this paternal act whole hog. For all I knew we were being played for suckers.

"We really should introduce ourselves," said the one in the bow tie. He appeared to have been pleasantly flustered by Sally's remark. "I'm Jeremy Clinton, Ph.D. I sit at Carrel G in Alcove Four. My field is Sanskrit, in particular its curious similarity to Southern American Negro patois with respect to...to, ah..."

"I'm Derek Bottomley, D.Mus., D.M.A., Carrel B, Alcove One. Music's my bailiwick. The history of batons—their function, construction and hidden symbolism. I think you'd be surprised to find out how many..."

"My name is Sigismund Krusinski, D.Mus., D.Ed.. I too am a servant of the Muse Euterpe. My carrel is right next to Doctor Bottomley's..." (They always referred to one another as "Doctor.")

"Actually, Sig, there's a water fountain between our desks. You can't really say that our carrels are *right next* to..."

"Yes, that's quite true, quite true, now that you mention it. Yes...In any event, the topic I've been researching for the past fifteen years is the incidence of baroque cadential trills in the early works of Constantine Perschel, whose splendid trio sonatas have traditionally—and, I would maintain, wrongly—been thought of as belonging to the Classical period. The thing to watch for, of course, is whether the appoggiatura..."

Not to be outdone by his colleagues, the fourth Bibliophile—Donald Snell, Doctor of Zoology and the Library's resident expert on the migratory habits of Tanzanian giraffes—at this point interrupted the third and launched into a protracted explanation of his favorite Library haunt and the nature of his labors. But the surrounding audience had by now grown restless and was beginning to chant little snatches of doggerel, such as: "Clear the rows, clear the aisles/Make way for the Bibliophiles!" and "Rational discourse, community of scholars,/We wouldn't trade our bridge team for a ton of federal dollars!" All of which convinced me that ours would be a lonely battle that day.

And lonely it was, for we had not one supporter in that room. But if I were to tell you that this first match was a life-and-death struggle or that the Bibliophiles turned out to have been masking, behind doddering personae, the most unbridled of competitive urges, I would be guilty of a gross distortion. It soon became obvious that the glint I had spied in the old men's eyes bespoke verve, intelligence and a childlike eagerness to learn, but not that predatory instinct which is part of every successful tournament player's makeup. Not that unabashed hunger to win. I was a fool to have been mistrustful. It was just as Sally had said. The Bibliophiles *were* the cuddliest little things that any of us had ever met.

Jeremy Clinton and Donald Snell, whom Reginald and I drew as opponents, held their own for the first fourteen deals, but we gave them a rather rough working over during the second half of that twenty-eight-board session. We played at the north end of the room and finished well ahead of the others (as I knew would be the case throughout this entire team competition due to La McGonigle's snaillike playing pace). Our opponents' partners then graciously invited us to watch the final few hands at the center table. "Please, gentlemen, feel free to join us," said Derek

Bottomley. "We don't stand on ceremony here. Besides, my colleagues and I know when we're being thrashed." Diggery, ever the gentleman, began protesting this last statement, and his lead was soon taken up by scores of the onlookers who, though they may have grown despondent in the face of their heroes' impending defeat, had nevertheless resolved to back them to the end.

No one in the audience regretted staying; for the final deal, while it could scarcely be characterized as the climax of the match, at least provided a satisfying denouement for everyone in the room but me:

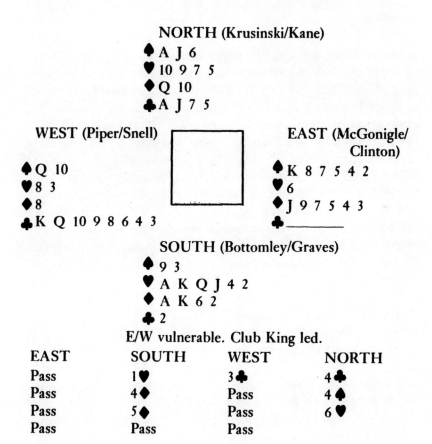

NORTH (Krusinski/Kane)
♠ A J 6
♥ 10 9 7 5
♦ Q 10
♣ A J 7 5

WEST (Piper/Snell)
♠ Q 10
♥ 8 3
♦ 8
♣ K Q 10 9 8 6 4 3

EAST (McGonigle/Clinton)
♠ K 8 7 5 4 2
♥ 6
♦ J 9 7 5 4 3
♣ _____

SOUTH (Bottomley/Graves)
♠ 9 3
♥ A K Q J 4 2
♦ A K 6 2
♣ 2

E/W vulnerable. Club King led.

EAST	SOUTH	WEST	NORTH
Pass	1♥	3♣	4♣
Pass	4♦	Pass	4♠
Pass	5♦	Pass	6♥
Pass	Pass	Pass	

How well I remember this hand. At the other table I'd sat North and Reginald South. The first seven bids went the same way there as here, including North's four-club cue bid to show first-round control of that suit along with a colossal heart fit. But I opted for Blackwood at my second opportunity, then took a fling at six notrump, knowing full well that we had long since wrapped up the match. A clubless East was on lead and sent a diamond around to my Queen-ten. I claimed my twelve tricks and gave the hand no further thought. "Should turn out fairly well," was all I'd said at the time to Reginald, who had simply shaken his head and smiled—in appreciation, I suppose, of my clever maneuvering of the bidding.

Now, if Bottomley and Krusinski had been as crafty, they would certainly have had an easier row to hoe. As it was, their surfeit of cue bids landed them in a six-heart contract which was dealt a baleful blow when at trick one Bottomley called for the Ace to cover Diggery's club King and Sally McGonigle ruffed. A groan of communal pain rose spontaneously from the audience as Derek Bottomley watched the odds on making his contract plummet from one hundred to fifty percent. And just as soon as Sally played back a spade to his Ace, Bottomley gathered in trumps in two rounds and led a diamond toward the ten in dummy with the purpose of taking that even-money gamble right off the bat. He would catch the Jack onside, or so he thought, and unload North's spade losers on his third and fourth diamond winners. But when Sally showed up with the missing diamond honor, he was through.

"Forget it, Derek," said Krusinski.

"Couldn't have been helped," consoled Snell.

"Really, Doctor Bottomley," said Sally, "you shouldn't be so upset. That Jack of mine was going to win whether you finessed or not."

"Just plain bad luck," agreed Clinton. "You certainly can't expect people to be holding eight-card suits."

"Actually that's not the point," I heard myself say. Once those words had escaped, an awkward silence fell over the canteen. Sally seemed puzzled, Reginald looked embarrassed, and the

110

Captain tried to warn me off with a threatening look.

"What do you mean, Mr. Kane?" Clinton asked. There was not the least trace of challenge in his voice.

"Well...nothing, really..."

"No, no. Go right ahead, please," said Bottomley, igniting a fresh pipe. "My colleagues and I are always anxious to pick up a pointer or two."

I was torn. On the one side there was Diggery's foreboding stare and the realization that what I had to say might possibly cause our hosts a modicum of discomfort. On the other side there was an audience of two hundred people—a far greater number than I had ever addressed—just waiting for me to share with them the fruits of my knowledge; perfectly primed, I could tell, to hear my version of that age-old lecture on the advisability of pausing before playing to the first trick. In the end my commitment to higher education tipped the balance.

"Well," said I, "Doctor Bottomley should have ducked the opening lead, regardless of how many clubs West figured to have for his preempt." I set the hand up for all to reexamine. The oohs and aahs of the audience, once they saw how that maneuver puts the contract in the bank, were gratifying indeed to the ears of one whose expertise had never before been so widely acknowledged.

"Why, he's absolutely right!" cried Bottomley.

"I must admit, it's a foolproof solution," seconded Snell with a diffident nod of the head. Then the kibitzers who were closer in began explaining to those on the periphery how the club Ace is thus preserved for South's spade loser once declarer captures the lead at the second trick and eliminates West's two trumps.

Sigismund Krusinski beamed at me and asked, "Am I correct in assuming that that's the way you played the hand at the other table?"

"No, sir," I answered. "I was North there, making six no trump, but I feel confident I would have employed that safety play had I been put to the test in six hearts..." If I had just had the good sense to stop there, I might have stridden from that snack bar in triumph, leaving two hundred seasoned games fanatics with the definite impression that the real star of the Piper Quartet was not

111

necessarily the player who had lent his name to that title. Yet the spotlight was mine and I would not be denied. "...But in all fairness, I should point out that if I'd been saddled with the six-heart contract and, through some lapse of concentration, had played high instead of low at trick one, I would have chosen the same line as Doctor Bottomley. That is, once I'd rejected the obvious alternative."

"Alternative?" asked Bottomley, snapping up the bait.

"Yes. Perhaps it would be helpful if we took another look at our cards..." You can see that I had hit my stride. Even the flash of quickening interest I detected in Diggery's eyes gave me no pause. "...Now, one of you might say: 'What's wrong with squeezing East in the pointed suits?' 'A good deal,' would be my reply. 'For you see, you cannot *overwork* East's hand' —oh, that's a bit of technical jargon used regularly on the tournament circuit to mean stretching an opponent's defensive resources beyond the breaking point—'with only six trump winners.' Here, watch what happens." I then demonstrated how after losing the ruff, winning the spade Ace and running trumps, South faces the following unsatisfactory position at trick nine:

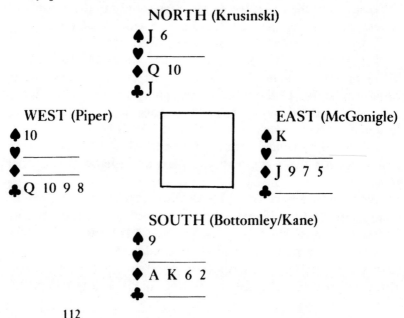

NORTH (Krusinski)
♠ J 6
♥ ———
♦ Q 10
♣ J

WEST (Piper)
♠ 10
♥ ———
♦ ———
♣ Q 10 9 8

EAST (McGonigle)
♠ K
♥ ———
♦ J 9 7 5
♣ ———

SOUTH (Bottomley/Kane)
♠ 9
♥ ———
♦ A K 6 2
♣ ———

"As you can clearly see, no one but declarer is in jeopardy. The best he can do is to throw East in with his spade and go off one. No, ladies and gentlemen," I summed up grandly, "the proper play is to finesse the diamond ten at trick five, just as Doctor Bottomley did. This allows you to bring in four diamond tricks and your contract whenever West has started out with the Jack."

"But what good does that do?" asked Sally with a wounded-poodle look. "The Jack's in the other hand."

"Right you are, my dear," said I with a knowing wink to my public. "In effect, the sole value of adopting that line of play is that you go down two tricks looking like an expert, instead of one trick looking like a fool." Everyone in the room, including the Bibliophiles themselves, acknowledged this paradox with a chuckle. Everyone, that is, except Diggery. He did manage a smile, but it was a very private smile. The smile, as I think back on it, of a stalking hunter who, even if he has not yet bagged his quarry, knows that the capture is inevitable.

"This has all been most enlightening," he began, "most enlightening, indeed. But before we leave—for it's well past tea time and we really must be moving along—I would like to propose that we play a round or two of that delightful children's game called . . . music chairs, is it?"

"Musical chairs!" corrected Krusinski and Bottomley in unison.

"Yes, that's it, musical chairs. In honor, shall we say, of our two music experts and our expert lecturer on bridge. To start, I will remain in the West seat. I will ask you, Doctor Bottomley, to become my partner as East and to cede the South seat, for the time being, to Mr. Kane. Doctor Krusinski, you will sit North, please . . . Now, is everyone ready?" No one, least of all I, knew what he was up to, but we were all in the mood to indulge him. He then beckoned us to pick up the hands that lay before us. The crowd moved in even closer than before to watch and listen to what was happening. "Here, I'll lead out the club King as I did earlier," Piper said, "and you, Doctor Krusinski, will please be kind enough to play the Ace again from dummy, keeping in mind the fact that Mr. Kane, were the decision his, would never commit such an egregious error. The trick is ruffed and South plays his

113

deuce." Piper rose dramatically from his seat. "Now if you will all move one position counterclockwise..." Once this was done, Diggery occupied the South seat with Bottomley across from him, Krusinski to his left, and me to his right. He then turned to me and said, "I believe it is your play."

"You're not suggesting that you can make this contract, are you?"

"Lead on," he grimly instructed. Piper was obviously more upset than I had thought. Was it simply a case of his feeling I'd been unduly harsh on Bottomley or was there a dark storm of envy roiling in his breast? Either way, he seemed to be letting his emotions get the better of him. I prepared to defend in the utmost confidence that my earlier analysis had fully accounted for this deal's intriguing possibilities.

"Well," I said, "I heard your side's cue bids as clearly as everyone else in this room. I know therefore that you hold the Ace-King of diamonds and that a lead at trick two away from my Jack gives away the contract via a free finesse. So I shift to a low spade, hoping my partner was dealt the Queen of that suit."

"As he was," said Piper, who captured Krusinski's Queen in dummy with his Ace. "You know," he continued, "you really have to learn to view things from the other chap's perspective."

I was beginning to chafe under the pressure of this public tongue-lashing, even though it must have been evident to everyone within earshot that the Captain was grossly overstating the damage my comments had done. "Look, I didn't mean what I said to Doctor Bottomley as an insult," I whispered, offering Piper a chance to save face.

"Oh, I wasn't referring to that," he protested. "Although, if the shoe fits, wear it. I meant that in the play of the hand, one must be flexible enough to shift one's point of view from time to time. He now called for the club five from the North hand—a tactic which had no apparent effect other than to substitute a ruff for a natural trump trick. When he did ruff, it was done in typical grandstand fashion with the Ace. "Now I lead a low trump to my ten and play another club." This time he ruffed with the King and led his meticulously preserved four of hearts to his nine. The Jack of

clubs was now ruffed with South's Queen, the trump Jack cashed
and the dummy reentered by way of the diamond Queen. Here
was the layout at that critical point:

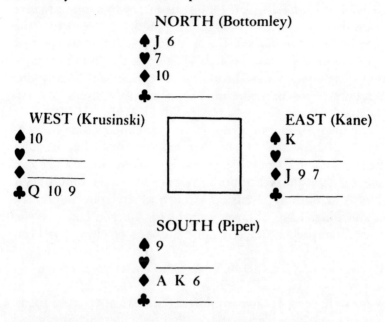

NORTH (Bottomley)
♠ J 6
♥ 7
♦ 10
♣ ———

WEST (Krusinski)
♠ 10
♥ ———
♦ ———
♣ Q 10 9

EAST (Kane)
♠ K
♥ ———
♦ J 9 7
♣ ———

SOUTH (Piper)
♠ 9
♥ ———
♦ A K 6
♣ ———

When Diggery called for the seven of hearts, my defenses crum-
bled like sand.

"How . . . how did you do that?" I stammered. Everyone around
me was looking on with equal fascination. Piper might have
levitated above the canteen floor and caused no greater a sensation.

"A rather basic example of dummy-reversal technique requiring nothing more complex than a change in one's frame of reference. Just the thing, really, for transforming six trump tricks into
seven."

"Extraordinary!" cried the Bibliophiles, looking and sounding
for all the world like a chorus of Doctor Watsons. The audience,
too, voiced its approval as I sat there blushing profusely.

"Terry," said Reginald, once the applause died down, "don't
you have something you want to say to Doctor Bottomley?"

115

"Yes...yes, I do. Doctor, I'm afraid I owe you an apology. I shouldn't have spoken out so rashly..." These words brought a bitter taste to my mouth—a taste I was determined to sweeten. "...I honestly believe that if I'd just had the opportunity to give the situation a moment's thought, I would have seen that the dummy reversal squeeze was the only way out of that fix and that your choice of the diamond finesse at trick five was just as ill conceived as your play of the club Ace at trick one. Clearly this contract can always be made, and I suppose it was careless of me to imply that..."

"Gentlemen," Piper interrupted, his peremptory tone conveying grave displeasure, "I see that my teammate hasn't quite learned his lesson. I would ask you all to rise once more and move to your right yet another position." Once that was accomplished I sat North as dummy, Krusinski South as declarer, Bottomley West and Piper East. "You now maintain, do you not, that the contract is impregnable even after the Ace of clubs has been ruffed?" he asked me.

"I...I certainly do. As you've just shown, all South has to do is..."

"Very well, then. I choose to shift at trick two not to a *low* spade but to the *King*. Now declarer, try what he will, must always go set." Alas, what he said was true. With the spade menace shifted to West, the squeeze on East evaporates and there is no way whatsoever to make the hand. Once again proved dead wrong, I rose from the North seat in dejection, only to find that my ordeal was still not at an end.

"Now *that*," said Sally McGonigle, "is my idea of how to reverse a dummy!" And her wisecrack brought the fool house down.

116

Episode X

In Which Bureaucrats and Strumpets Fall Beneath the Wheels of the Quartet's Juggernaut...
(February through June, 1983)

That drastic a setback would no doubt have destroyed a lesser man's morale. But I bounced back, resilient as ever, and regained my fighting form well before our next match. This is hardly to say that I entertained no doubts as to the effect of this spy mission on my general psychic health; or that I did not begin to experience at least as many lows of regret as highs of excitement following our victory over the Bibliophiles. I craved the prestige that was already starting to come our way, and still derived intense satisfaction from the knowledge that I was serving my country. But I resented the way my co-agents tended to keep me in the dark, and—a far more troublesome concern—I missed Jane, my privacy, the quiet life.

"What do we care about your inner emotional state?" the bridge hounds among you are probably baying "Quit dawdling and get on with it!"

They may well have a point. But if I am guilty of procrastinating, it is because, quite honestly, I find myself confronted with the first technical problem I have encountered in the writing of this diary (which activity, up to this point at least, has been both

117

pleasurable and surprisingly therapeutic). I must now take on what I have always regarded as the most difficult and least appreciated task of playwrights, novelists, scenarists, composers of journals—of all storytellers, in fact, the breadth of whose subject requires an occasional detour from detailed incident to a tight encapsulation of plot. The three creative writing seminars I attended during my fifth year in graduate school did not deal with how to make such Procrustean beds. Nor have I ever found a label for this device in the entire lexicon of literary criticism. Back in my teaching days at Sibley High I dubbed it "The Time-Passes Ploy."

It takes the inventiveness of an Orson Welles to make time pass with style. I will not even mention those arrogant fiction writers and dramatists who think they're getting away with something when they leapfrog five or ten years by slapping a date onto a chapter heading or onto an act/scene notation in a playbill. No, I refer you instead to the filmmaker's art, where this problem of time-telescoping must often be solved in purely visual terms. There are, of course, devices for hours, devices for months, devices for years. How many times, dear reader, have you sat before a screen and watched the hands of a clock spin madly around the dial, then stop five minutes shy of the time when a leader is to be assassinated, an enemy trench attacked, or a major urban center blown to smithereens? How many times have you been treated to a close-up of a day calendar on a bare wall, its pages falling away slowly at first, like dying leaves, then briskly, like snowflakes in a blizzard, until September is transformed into December? How many times have you flicked on an oldie dating from the thirties or forties and, halfway through, stared at the pulsating drums of a giant printing press as headlines kept zooming at you right off page one, and an orchestral brass section blared a progression of tragic chords, and the jut-jawed face of the hero (a swell guy imprisoned for what you and he knew was a bum rap) remained hauntingly superimposed over the entire affair?

Primitive mechanisms, you will say. Ah, but when Citizen and Mrs. Kane take their montage of breakfasts in that one truly immortal Time-Passes sequence, and the gradual deterioration of

118

their marriage is delicately and plausibly documented in fewer than one hundred seconds, who resents the artifice? Who begrudges the storyteller his blatant intrusion?

If I had felt my own humble talent were sufficiently refined to carry off such legerdemain, I would never have come out into the open like this. But I frankly admit that the sixteen matches and five months of Grand National competition that passed between the time of our victory over the Bibliophiles and the climactic battles to be recounted in Episodes XI and XII of this chronicle were relatively drab by comparison. Not, I hasten to explain, because the opponents we faced were any less interesting than the good doctors at the Library, or because the quality of play was that much less scintillating than what we encountered in our matches during July and August, but because the element of suspense, so constant a factor during our last two contests, was never much in evidence. The Piper Quartet was quite simply too strong.

I will not be so cavalier as to peel away the calendar pages between late January and early July, but I will limit myself nonetheless to reporting only the highlights of two of our contests—those against the Foggy Bottom Bombers and the notorious Knockout Knockouts.

I am proud to report that I was the star of the deal that doused the Bombers' faint hopes. Those four State Department employees were given a lesson that day in point-counting that they are not likely soon to forget. Here is the hand and the bidding, which was identical at both tables:

NORTH (Graves)
♠ 10 9
♥ K 6 4
♦ J 9 3 2
♣ A Q 6 5

WEST
♠ K Q
♥ 10 8 7 3
♦ 7 6 5 4
♣ J 8 4

EAST
♠ 7 4 3
♥ Q 9
♦ A Q 10 8
♣ K 10 3 2

SOUTH (Kane/Seedyke)
♠ A J 8 6 5 2
♥ A J 5 2
♦ K
♣ 9 7

E/W vulnerable. Diamond four led.

EAST	SOUTH	WEST	NORTH
Pass	1 ♠	Pass	2 ♣
Pass	2 ♥	Pass	2 ♠
Pass	3 ♠	Pass	Pass
Pass			

"So you've got a loser in each suit. What's the problem?" Yes, I am prepared to hear comments such as these ring out from the result merchants among you who, when presented with a printed deal, never cover up the East and West holdings but tailor their declarer play to what they see in all four hands. Yet Graham Seedyke, the Bomber who played this deal at one end of the State Department's ceremonial ballroom, and yours truly, who played it at the other, did not enjoy the luxury of scrutinizing the distribution of the enemy trump suit. From where we sat, repeated spade finesses against East looked like the most likely way to avoid losing two tricks in that suit.

Thus when Seedyke did just that and lost to both spade honors, he cursed the gods of chance. In reality he had committed the

120

fourth of Piper's Seven Deadly Sins: "The Playing of One Suit As If It Bore No Relation to the Length, Texture and Quality of the Other Three."

West made the opening lead of a diamond against me, just as Diggery did against Seedyke at the other table. In both cases East's Ace felled South's King. Now East shifted to a trump, which appeared to be the only safe lead. Both Seedyke and I played low. West captured the trick with a deceitful King and continued diamonds from the safe side; but here the two declarers parted company. Seedyke called for the three from dummy and ruffed it in hand, lost the club finesse, won the club continuation with North's Ace, then ventured a second unsuccessful finesse in the trump suit. Well before the man's protestations of hard luck stopped echoing in the great bannered hall, Sally and the Captain had salted away the heart trick that put him down one.

Certainly it is upsetting when a three-out-of-four shot fails to come in, but what Piper taught me to see is that a seventy-five percent chance *in vacuo* will often turn out to be a very poor bet in context. Observe.

When my West opponent pushed a second diamond at the third trick, I called not for the three but for the Jack, just to satisfy myself that East had indeed started with the Ace-Queen of that suit, as the defense up to that point suggested. Then, once I ruffed the Queen, lost the club finesse to East's King, and was put up in dummy with the club Ace at trick five, I paused to add. ("For cursed above all be they," Diggery had warned us at the end of lesson nine, "who, though having fingers, will not count.") Hadn't East contributed an Ace, a King and a Queen to the first five tricks? Why rush to take the second trump hook? Why not first finesse in hearts and add one more brushstroke to the emerging portrait of the count? And sure enough, when my Jack won and East was revealed as the possessor of the Queen, I held enough evidence to deduce that West had originally been dealt both key trumps. For how many East players holding thirteen high-card points would have initiated the bidding with a pass?

I tabled the Ace of spades, virtually assured that if West had begun with a doubleton, I would now drop the Queen, and that if

121

he'd begun with the King-Queen-low, there would never have been any way of avoiding two losers. My circumspection was repaid in full, for the trump Queen fell and the partial was made.

As I pointed out earlier, the five-IMP swing that resulted from this tidy little piece of detection was hardly a *sine qua non* of our victory over the Bombers. The deal is offered merely as an indication of how seriously I was taking this Grand National competition; of how religiously I had heeded my Captain's wise entreaties; of how carefully I now played in comparison to the days when the stakes were not world peace but some fraction of a masterpoint.

With the hope of demonstrating that Reginald too had attained a new peak of performance, I will next relate a deal drawn from our June 16 set-to with a team representing the capital's infamous red-light district. The Knockout Knockouts, as they call themselves, are four free-lance salespersons who work the Fourteenth Street strip between K and T, dispensing a wide variety of services for a fairly uniform price of forty dollars, and who happen to spend a great deal of their leisure time playing bridge. The match took place at 7:30 A.M. on the virtually windowless top floor of a four-story walk-up—a building commonly known in Washington as a "tourist home." That time was chosen so as not to interfere with our opponents' business hours, which stretched from noon until three in the morning.

The Knockouts introduced themselves simply as Ruby, Esmeralda, Scarlet and Bunny. (I would have given anything to see the face of the Grand National functionary who processed their registration form.) Our ambassador of goodwill took over from there.

"Wow!" said Sally as she groped her way toward a threadbare armchair in the faded rose half-light of that room. "It sure is dark in here."

"Hey, tha's the way the johns like it, Red."

Sally, whose eyes had not yet adjusted to the dim interior, gave a start at the sound of this voice. Within seconds a Cheshire-cat grin materialized, then a ravenous pair of eyes glinting beneath the brim of a gray felt fedora. "Who...who are you?"

"Me? I'm Chick."

"But what are you doing here?"

"Look, somebody's gotta run this show, right?"

"It's okay, darling," Scarlet assured Sally. "He's sort of our nonplaying captain." Then, turning to the man: "Chick, the reason these people are here is..."

"What am I, some kinda school kid? I know what they're here for." He indicated by nodding that Sally should sit down. She did so and returned his leer with a prim little smile, all the while staring at his thickly muscled frame, which was encased like country sausage in a white linen jumpsuit, and at the two diamond pinkie rings which, when canted at a certain angle, reflected the room's pale, penumbral glow.

"Well," said Sally in an attempt to break the ice, "are the Johns the people who usually play here?"

"The johns're the people who *always* play here."

"I see. And they like it this dark, huh?" Sally glanced at the rest of us and giggled nervously. "Now me, I'm used to a well-lit room. Especially when I'm getting ready for a three- or four-hour session..." (Here Chick's eyes bulged in amazement.) "...But heck, I'll try anything once. Just seems like it'd be pretty tough to see what the Sam Hill was going on when you were turning your tricks."

"You like to see what's goin' on, do you, Red?"

"You bet I do! Shoot, you could easily mistake a Queen for a Jack in here."

"It's not a jack, babe, it's a john. And this is a straight operation. You ain't gonna find no queens up here."

"You're kidding! No Queens at all?"

Chick now looked in our direction for help.

"Miss Sally," said Piper, "why don't we just drop this and..."

"What else don't you allow?" she continued.

"Well, I like to think I'm pretty loose about the rest of it. Tell you what, you ask me and I'll let you know if it's allowed."

"Okay. Let's start with deuces."

"Whoa! See, now you're talkin' about female business. They're

123

okay, I guess—'specially the disposable kind—in case somethin' goes wrong with a rubber."

"Well, now there's a silly rule, if you ask me. What could possibly go wrong with a rubber? Anyway, I thought there weren't going to be any rubbers today. I thought we were going to play duplicate."

"Jesus," said Bunny.

"Look, Red, don't go tryin' to tell me how to run my own joint, okay? I'm already stretchin' the rules just by lettin' you up here with these three jokers. There's no way you're gonna do this funky 'duplicate' number, or whatever you call it, with any of my girls."

"All right, but how about those deuces?"

"Like I said, tha's up to you, woman. Use 'em if you want to. All I'm sayin' is, rubbers're a house rule. Got it?"

"Fair enough," replied Sally, flashing the triumphant smile of a negotiator who has just extracted a key concession. "No duplicate and no Queens, but deuces are optional. I guess I can live with that arrangement. Well, what're we waiting for? Let's get started!... Oh, by the way, Chick, if you get the urge to take the place of one of the ladies after an hour or so, I'm sure none of my friends'd object." Reginald, Diggery and I smiled sheepishly.

"Chick," Ruby interrupted, just when matters threatened to take a nasty turn, "would you come over here a minute? There's something I think you should know."

Following that intriguing bit of chitchat (which, but for its surreal quality, should never have been accorded precious space in this Time-Passes episode), Graves and I moved to a room down the hall and squared off against Bunny and Esmeralda, leaving Piper and McGonigle to contend with Ruby, Scarlet and the Knockouts' burly chaperone. Nothing of much note occurred at the latter table, other than the commotion Sally caused when she was dealt the Queen of spades, the Queen of diamonds and the Queen of clubs on the very first hand. It was rather in our room that the issue was decided; for during the first ten deals, my partner and I built up a lead that proved to be insurmountable. There were minor swings this way and that for the remainder of

the contest, but the Quartet was never once in serious trouble.
Here is the hand I have chosen to showcase Reginald's prowess:

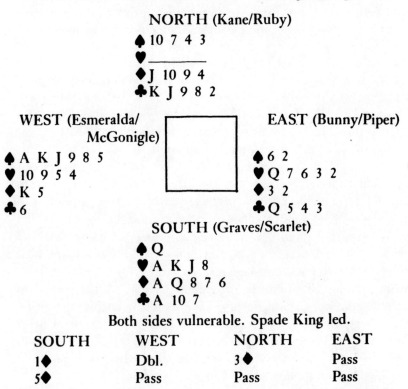

NORTH (Kane/Ruby)
♠ 10 7 4 3
♥ ————
♦ J 10 9 4
♣ K J 9 8 2

WEST (Esmeralda/
McGonigle)
♠ A K J 9 8 5
♥ 10 9 5 4
♦ K 5
♣ 6

EAST (Bunny/Piper)
♠ 6 2
♥ Q 7 6 3 2
♦ 3 2
♣ Q 5 4 3

SOUTH (Graves/Scarlet)
♠ Q
♥ A K J 8
♦ A Q 8 7 6
♣ A 10 7

Both sides vulnerable. Spade King led.

SOUTH	WEST	NORTH	EAST
1♦	Dbl.	3♦	Pass
5♦	Pass	Pass	Pass

We later learned that Scarlet—who was dealt the South hand in
the adjoining room—drove the bidding, as Reginald did, to the
five-diamond level. Having lost the opening spade lead and a
subsequent trump finesse, she approached the crucial club situation at trick six as a fifty-fifty proposition. She did try to improve
her chances by resorting to a time-worn sucker play: with the look
of someone in the act of finessing, she called for the Jack from
dummy. Fortunately the Captain and not Sally was sitting East.
Piper—whom I have never once seen cover an honor that did not
deserve covering—smoothly turned down this come-on. And so
Scarlet overtook the Jack with her Ace and ran the ten. Down one.

125

But notice how Reginald converted what appears to be a guess into an absolute certainty. The bidding at our table was very short and very sweet, my three-diamond preemptive call over West's double neatly clearing the path for Reginald's charge into game. Esmeralda took the opening trick with the King of spades, but Reginald then ruffed her Ace with the trump six. Those two tricks, as well as the following three, in fact, were played virtually the same way in both rooms. A heart was now ruffed in the North hand and a losing diamond finesse taken. The trump five was next captured in dummy by Scarlet and in the closed hand by Graves. But now instead of turning immediately to the clubs, as his counterpart did, Reginald harkened back to the urging of our spiritual leader—"Never underestimate the benefits that accrue to the declarer who knows all twenty-six of the opposition's cards"—and set about the task of determining the count. At that early stage the picture was indeed unclear, for Esmeralda and Bunny had each played two spades, one heart and two diamonds. Even when Reginald cashed his Ace and King of hearts, both women followed suit. (My provident partner, by the way, was careful here not to sluff both of his apparently useless spades on those heart winners. One was saved for later.) Now came the heart Jack, which Graves ruffed in dummy with his ten. Neither opponent had yet shown out of anything. But when that carefully retained ten of spades was led in this position:

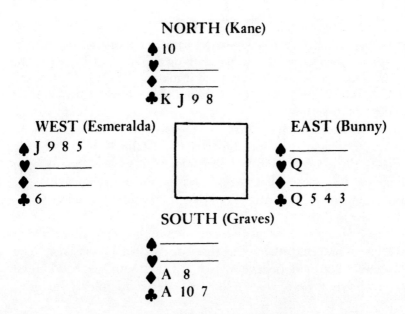

NORTH (Kane)
♠ 10
♥ _____
♦ _____
♣ K J 9 8

WEST (Esmeralda)
♠ J 9 8 5
♥ _____
♦ _____
♣ 6

EAST (Bunny)
♠ _____
♥ Q
♦ _____
♣ Q 5 4 3

SOUTH (Graves)
♠ _____
♥ _____
♦ A 8
♣ A 10 7

it was all over but for the shuffling. Bunny did her best to thwart the sly discovery play by sluffing a club instead of the thirteenth heart, which would have given everything away; but as it was, Reginald knew as much as he needed to know. He might have laid down his trump Ace now and completed the tally, but he opted instead for a subtler alternative.

"Let's see," he mused aloud, taking a page out of Diggery's book, "if East was dealt only two spades, then West must have started out with six. And six spades, plus four hearts, plus two diamonds makes twelve. I believe I can claim now, ladies. I play a low club to my King, you see, and if Esmeralda's one unknown card turns out to be anything but the Queen of that suit, I take the marked finesse one trick later against Bunny."

"Cute..." said Esmeralda, brushing a platinum blond tress back in place. "...A little *too* cute."

In retrospect, I am ready to admit that Esmeralda had just cause for complaint. But a certain amount of cockiness, I have found, naturally accompanies as dramatic an improvement in technique as my partner and I had effected. Even if our play could not yet be labeled inspired or placed in the same category as that of the Captain's, we were nonetheless making a solid contribution to the team's soaring fortunes. What did it matter if we'd become just a bit overconfident? Hadn't we proved that we could back up our words with action?

But little did we know that our months of coasting had come to an end and that the Piper Quartet had chalked up its last easy victory in a long skein of landslide results. We should have realized, I suppose, that as time passes, the going must at some point get rough. Yet before we knew it, the intoxicating victories of winter and spring were history, the district playoffs were upon us, and we were on our way to a match with a team about whom we knew nothing other than that they called themselves "The Caucus." You may believe me when I say that if we had known then who they were, we would have sobered up quickly enough.

128

Episode XI

In Which a King Proves Nothing to Sneeze at...
(July 7, 1983)

It is four o'clock in the afternoon and I break from my narrative to reflect upon the view now offered me. Ferries and barges chug down the river, sending out coal-black whorls of smoke and hornblasts muffled by the far-off racket of the city. The city, where taxicabs alternately crawl and careen along the crosshatch of avenues and streets, and where untold millions march down the sidewalks like armies of sea-bent lemmings. This was the quintessential hour (or so my friends back home had told me) to observe the wonder that is Manhattan—in the broad light of a weekday afternoon, when the island's machinery is churning at full throttle and its skyscrapers teem with human occupation. But judging from my own marathon vigil, it is above all in the eerie glow of dawn that the power and vitality of that mammoth metropolis come into graphic relief.

You will accuse me, reader, of projecting onto the view my feelings of isolation; and to some extent I know this must be true. For the first time in my life I am a lonely man. My mind wanders. I daydream and feel sorry for myself. I resent the most inoffensive displays of affection on the part of lovers spied in public places;

129

seethe with envy at the chance meeting of friends unknown to me; am haunted by the realization that throughout the length and breadth of that bedlam across the river, there breathes not one human being in whom I can confide. And that includes, it pains me to admit, my teammates.

There was a day not so very long ago (the 29th of April, if I recall correctly) when I would not have made so sweeping a charge. When Reginald Graves at long last breached the wall of silence which, ever since the night I'd flushed the Captain and his confederates from their den, had shielded me from any hard facts surrounding our mysterious mission.

"Reginald," I remember saying to him over lunch at a quaint little Capitol Hill restaurant called the Patio Café, "I've just got to know more about what we're supposed to be doing. For my own peace of mind, if for no other reason. I can't stand all this secrecy." At first he tried to sidetrack me, as usual, with a barrage of irrelevant information and alluring promises. He spoke of unlimited expense accounts, of upcoming matches in Philadelphia, New York, San Francisco, of luxury suites at the Plaza and the Sir Francis Drake, of the need to secure a leave of absence from my job.

"A leave of absence from the mailroom? But I couldn't possibly get away now. We're coming up to the election rush. There'll be hundreds of photographs and pen sets and complimentary American flags going out to every congressional constituency from the start of the major primaries, next Tuesday, until the first week of November."

"I'm afraid someone else will have to take care of it," Reginald said. "You're part of this operation now, Terry, even if it wasn't planned that way."

"But what will I live on?"

"Oh, don't worry about the financial side of things. Tomorrow morning your first salary payment will be dropped off at your apartment. In cash, of course. If there's any problem with the amount, just let me know about it. But remember, you're to tell no one about this—not Internal Revenue, not your friends, no one."

"What would I know to say?" I asked sarcastically.

130

"You're dissatisfied about something?"

"You bet I am. I'm dissatisfied that I can't seem to get a straight answer to my questions out of you or Diggery."

"Fire away," he said with a hunch of the shoulders, as if I'd never before bothered to ask.

"Does this mission . . ." Here Reginald raised a hand to deter me from continuing until the waitress—an arthritic, bandy-legged matron who could have passed as my grandmother—set down a platter of scrambled eggs and sausage and tottered off. "Does this mission have a name?"

"Operation Endplay," he answered without a hitch.

"How did you and Sally get tied up in it?"

"That's easy. Our committee jobs give us access to relevant intelligence data and offer a convenient excuse for foreign travel, for instance when we had to go overseas to be trained and briefed by European-based NATO officials. Plus, Sally and I both happen to play a little bridge."

"That's another thing. Just exactly how does bridge enter into it, anyway? If you recall, Diggery never got very specific back in January as to the nature of the bridge connection."

"All right, here's how it is. We're dealing, my friend, with a network of agents without a country. A lawless pack of renegades who bargain for sensitive military intelligence, then auction it off to the highest bidder. For years now the marketplace for this trade has been the Spingold, Reisinger, Grand National and World Olympiad competitions. Twice before this, Interpol cadres have tried to break the ring by infiltrating tournaments. Twice they failed."

"What went wrong?"

"I imagine you've read about the famous scandal at the 1965 World Team Championships in Buenos Aires involving two English experts accused of . . ."

"Flashing finger signals to communicate their heart holdings? Who hasn't?"

"Well, those gestures were signals, all right, but they had nothing to do with hearts. Then there was the Italian fiasco of 1975."

"Don't tell me the foot-nudging brouhaha in Bermuda was part of all this?"

"Interpol squad number two," he explained calmly. "In both cases our plants were detected, then exposed, by overly observant members of the United States press corps who had no idea of how far back they were setting the cause of worldwide nuclear saf——I mean, of worldwide accord."

"What?" I cried. "Weren't you about to say 'worldwide nuclear safety'?"

"Quiet!" he commanded. Surely he was overreacting. The only potential eavesdroppers were the party of teenaged diners sitting in the booth next to ours, and they seemed far more interested in bolting their cheeseburgers and French fries than in listening to anything Reginald and I had to say. "The phrase I used was 'worldwide *accord.*' Remember that. If the Captain finds out I told you even that much I could get scrubbed from the project."

I was grateful indeed for this show of candor. Although there was never one iota of follow-up, that briefing session proved, at the time, to be just the boost I needed for my lagging spirits. I decided, on an impulse, to repay honesty with honesty; to divulge my long-kept secret.

"Now I've got something to tell you," I said with a coy smile.

"Oh? What's that?"

"I know about the microdots."

For a very long time, Reginald was silent. For a very long time, his mouth hung open and his eyes stared, incredulous, into mine. Finally he stammered, "What did you say?"

"I . . . I said I know about the microdots. I heard Diggery mention them that night on the Capitol ellipse. It's all right, Reginald. I'm discreet about things like this."

"Wait here," he ordered, following another rather annoying pause, then dashed off toward a phone booth in the back room. When he returned, he refused to say a word more. He just sat there poking nervously at his omelet.

Ten minutes later a parrotless Diggery Piper entered the Patio Café and pulled up a seat at our table. He was smiling, but it was one of those smiles that hide far more than they reveal.

132

"Now, Terence, what's all this business about microdots?"

"I don't know. I mean, I didn't realize it was such a big deal."

"Reginald tells me you overheard a bit more of a rather sensitive discussion than you originally let on. Is that so?" He was still smiling, but a muscle in his right cheek seemed to twitch intermittently with strain.

"Well, yes. I guess I should have mentioned it back then."

"What *exactly* did you hear? And this time, do try to be thorough, won't you?"

"I just heard someone—I think it was you—use the word 'microdot,' that's all."

"Nothing more, old boy?"

"No. I swear it."

"And what, pray tell, do you understand by this term 'microdot'? In the context of my profession, that is."

"It's...it's a disk, isn't it?" I asked, all but choking on the thickness in my throat. "A tiny disk on which you can fit whole documents in microfilm form."

"Precisely, And what connection do you believe such disks have with our enemies?"

"I don't know. I guess I assumed from what you told me later that night that they—the people in the spy ring—probably used microdots in the past to convey stolen intelligence secrets."

"And that was a very astute assumption," said Piper. "A very astute assumption indeed."

"Do you expect them to use them again this time?" I was emboldened by what I interpreted as a slight thaw in the Captain's attitude.

"Well now, we don't want to go about dispensing information indiscriminately, do we? Each of us—even I, mind you—knows only as much as he or she needs to know in order to function at a level of optimal efficiency. Regrettably, though perhaps unavoidably, you have upset the delicate balance. Now, I am not saying that this constitutes sufficient grounds to expel you from the cadre. We need you, Terence. You've got talents and personality traits that dovetail perfectly with the exigencies of our operation. But do not make the mistake of thinking that you have somehow

133

become indispensable to the mission's success."

"No, I don't. I don't think that at all."

"Then please refrain in the future from prying into matters that do not directly concern you. Understood?"

"Understood."

"Fine, then. All's forgotten. Now tell me, can you recommend the fish and chips?"

And so I hunkered down, reminding myself that, as difficult as it was, I was finally doing something important. Something that mattered. (Wasn't this the reason, after all, why I'd abandoned my niche in the Boston school system and moved household and hopes to the capital?) Yes, I did as Piper requested. I buttoned up, thus banishing myself once again to this limbo of virtual isolation.

Reginald's promise of travel panned out soon enough, although our first trips hardly proved exotic. A good many of the Quartet's battles thereafter were fought away from home against teams in Virginia, Maryland, Delaware and Pennsylvania—all of which territory, according to the 1980 revised tournament structure, fell within the Mid-Atlantic States division of the Grand National's northeast zone. But our opponents outside the borders of the district fared no better against us than had the Bibliophiles, the Foggy Bottom Bombers or the Knockout Knockouts. And so by early July, only one team in that entire jurisdiction stood between us and a shot at the zonal championship. The survivor of the match between the Piper Quartet and this mystery team called "The Caucus" would go on to challenge the New York–New England division winner in a showdown at Manhattan's Plaza Hotel. I had never been to the Plaza. I had never even been to New York City. I was determined to win.

Equally determined, if for far different reasons (reasons which I, too, shared to a lesser extent) were Graves, McGonigle and the Captain. It was with a collective expression of grim resolve that the four of us sat in the Jefferson Lounge on the evening of July 7 and awaited the visiting team's arrival.

I could tell from the start that something was wrong. The

Quartet had arranged to use the club only twice before in the course of the tournament: once, in late February, against the IRS Taxonomists and once, a month later, against a team hailing from Laurel, Maryland. On both those nights our fellow club members had rooted us on to victory with an unabashed display of partisanship. Tonight, although a full house waited for play to begin, the mood was very different. David Johnson, chief counsel on the Senate Foreign Relations Committee, came over to wish Sally and the rest of us good luck; and my mailroom boss, Gloria Schaffner (to whom I had that day submitted my application for a two-month leave of absence) did the same. Yet no other member offered any but the most perfunctory signs of support. At first I thought this shocking lack of enthusiasm might have been due to the fact that the four of us had not competed in the club's regular Monday-night game since embarking on our heavy tournament schedule; or, more likely, that the crowd's cool civility was merely a natural reaction to the tense vibrations which my partners and I were emitting. But when the door to the anteroom suddenly burst open, that comatose gallery of ninety-odd people leaped to its feet and welcomed our opponents with a tumultuous hometown cheer.

Like ghosts from the past did the four Caucus members weave and wend their way about the room. And as they paraded, my long-time friends and colleagues in the club cried, "Get 'em, Buttergut!" and "You can do it, Penelope!" and "Show 'em how, Tight Fist!" and "Win one for us, Obadiah!" Even when the answer to the enigma lay before me, the reality of the situation was at first too monstrous to accept. But soon there was no denying it: Parker, Gumpers, Steinkamp and Crawley would be our adversaries that night. If I was ever to see the legendary sights of Gotham, the Piper Quartet would have to outplay a man who, for all his military mumble-jumble, had won the club championship the past twelve years running; a woman whose professed disdain for published analyses of "highfalutin gadgets" and "fancy-Dan plays" was surpassed only by her instinctive comprehension of such niceties; a clever old codger who'd waged a lifelong battle against overdrafts and overtricks alike; and a conservative politi-

135

cian who took a decidedly liberal attitude toward the laws governing contract bridge. It would be difficult enough to defeat such a perfectly matched set of misfits with both sides playing at equal advantage, but the Caucus had the crowd behind them. Nor did it come as any surprise that this silver-haired foursome, representing an accumulated eighty-seven years of Congressional Club affiliation, would exert a far stronger claim on the loyalty of the membership than would the band of relative upstarts with whom I was aligned.

Round and round the room they marched, with Major Parker out in front calling his famous hut-hut beat and the pathetic Mortimer Fisk, pressed into service as a cheerleader, inspiring the gallery to ever greater heights of frenzy. A good five minutes passed before Edmund Gradys at last called the proceedings to order and directed the two teams to sit down and decide who would play against whom. Now, as has been documented in this journal, there was no lack of bad blood in our past. The Caucus players in particular showed no reluctance at all to air their feelings of personal rivalry and—I can find no delicate way to put it—their lust for personal revenge.

"I never have forgotten that cheap double squeeze you pulled on me last October," said Crawley to the Captain in his gruff, throaty voice. "I've been waiting a long time for a head-to-head rematch."

"I've got no beef with him," said Buttergut, the muscles of his stomach twitching with anticipation. "It's the redhead, there, that gets my goat. She took more top boards away from me this year than you can count jowls on a hog."

"Well that's certainly agreeable to us," replied Diggery on behalf of himself and Sally, who appeared somewhat taken aback by the Major's taste in metaphors.

"Suits me right to the ground," said Penelope Gumpers, and she looked straight at me as she spoke. "I've been itching to pay this one back ever since he helped the McGonigle girl rob me of a sure trump trick against a slam contract last November. 'Course he was my partner at the time."

"He was mine a month later," lamented Steinkamp. "Wrecked a spade game by turning down a diamond finesse every novice and

136

his mother would've taken. The fellow over there with the funny pants and the parrot said it was a 'McGonigle Coup' or something. I say it was just plain stupid."

On and on went the verbal abuse, but the four of us met these barbs with indifference. For a cardplayer's indulgence in diatribe, like a Lothario's indulgence in liquor, quite often proves counterproductive. And so it appeared to be that day. Whether it was indeed because our opponents' judgment was fogged by the intensity of their ego investment or because we were actually the stronger team, Reginald and I played Gumpers and Steinkamp even, during the first half of the match, while Sally and Diggery blitzed Crawley and Parker. "The Piper Quartet, by thirty-one IMPs," announced Gradys during the midpoint break for refreshments, whereupon the lounge was filled with gasps of near despair.

But in the second half it was a different story at both tables. In truth Graves and I did not do too badly. Steinkamp and Gumpers, still stunned by the vast improvement they'd seen in our play during the first fourteen deals, never completely recovered. Even though they had the upper hand, the damage they inflicted on us was so negligible that we assumed the match was ours. Yet that was before we learned of the fireworks exploding in the main room. Of how the Congressman and the Major had abandoned all caution in favor of a desperate two-pronged attack. Parker, we were soon to learn, had been forcing the bidding beyond the limits of his partnership's point count in the hopes that a modicum of luck and his own formidable declarer play might generate a rash of favorable swings. His partner, in the meantime, had launched an all-out legalistic campaign calculated to win back through nit-picking directorial decisions those losses which could not be fully recouped by dint of talent.

Once Gumpers, Steinkamp, Reginald and I had completed play in the anteroom, we were permitted to take seats among the gallery in the lounge. The evening's second-to-last deal was just being bid. It was during that uneventful partial (I remember it as a cut-and-dried two-spade affair) that I quietly asked Vera von Danzig, press secretary to an obscure Michigan Congressman, to summarize the highlights of the previous twelve boards' action.

"Major Lucks Out Twice In Inferior Slams..." she answered in a staccato whisper. "...Suspect Solon Uses Rulebook To Advantage."

"Once again?" Capitol Hill fairly crawls with media-crazed press aides but few take their jobs as much to heart as Vera. Nothing pleases the woman more than to conduct an entire conversation in the elliptical, upper-case exclamatory lingo which crowns her daily crop of releases. There have been times when I've been in the mood to humor her (my subscriptions to *Variety* and the Sunday edition of the *New York Daily News* certainly enable me to bandy headlines with the best of them), but this was not one of those occasions. Picking up on this immediately, she reverted to a low-key reportorial drone.

"...At 10:24 this evening, Major Winthrop "Buttergut" Parker bid a twenty-seven-point, six-spade vulnerable slam which had an eleven-percent chance of making...The portly Pentagonian brought that contract home when he found his East opponent's King-Jack-nine-seven of spades conveniently located in front of his Ace-Queen-ten-eight-six and played him for that holding...Estimated net gain, eleven IMPs...Three hands later, Parker huddled for two and one half minutes before dropping a singleton offside King to bring in an improbable three-notrump game...Estimated net gain, seven IMPs..."

"You don't think they've made up the difference, do you?" I asked her. But there is no polite way to interrupt Vera von Danzig once she is launched on one of her Walter Winchell spiels. She just churns out item after item, much like the electronic news message that used to run around the top of the Allied Chemical Building in Times Square.

"...Congressman Obadiah Crawley, whose alleged use of grins, grimaces and other facial contortions was earlier objected to unsuccessfully by his opponents, secured three favorable rulings during the second half of the match from director Edmund Gradys...All three infractions involved hesitations on the part of Miss Sally McGonigle—hesitations which, to this reporter, ap-

138

peared all but imperceptible... The first instance occurred at 10:17, when..."

I listened, enraged, as Vera recounted the details of that scoundrel's campaign of harassment. It is common knowledge at the Congressional Club that Sally McGonigle hesitates before every single bid and every single play—including the thirteenth trick—and that since those uniform, five-second-long pauses occur like clockwork, they convey no information either to her partner or to the opposition. But technically, I suppose, she has always left herself open to accusations that her delays communicate bidding or defensive clues, or at least that they slow the game down inordinately. According to Vera, Crawley had seen to it that penalties were assessed on both counts. It was exasperating enough that the Caucus had garnered a stack of IMPs as a direct result of such bush-league ploys, but at trick one of the very hand I was now only half watching, Sally became so flustered by the Congressman's hostile tactics that she led out of turn, thereby allowing Buttergut Parker to rake in two overtricks and another pair of IMPs.

"...Well, that about wraps things up here at the Jefferson Lounge, pending of course the outcome of the final board, which is even now being..."

"Thank you, Vera, thank you. That'll do just fine."

"What did she say?" asked Reginald as Crawley, Parker, Piper and McGonigle began studying the cards you see here:

139

NORTH (Crawley)
♠ 10 4 2
♥ A 10
♦ J 7 6
♣ K J 10 8 3

WEST (Piper)
♠ 9 8 6 5 3
♥ 7 6 4 2
♦ 4
♣ A 9 4

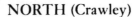

EAST (McGonigle)
♠ A 7
♥ K J 9 8
♦ Q 10 9 8 3
♣ Q 2

SOUTH (Parker)
♠ K Q J
♥ Q 5 3
♦ A K 5 2
♣ 7 6 5

Both vulnerable. Spade five led.

SOUTH	WEST	NORTH	EAST
1NT	Pass	3NT	Pass
Pass	Pass		

"Bad news," I whispered. "Crawley and Parker may've pulled the Caucus even by now. What happened against Steinkamp and Gumpers on this hand, do you remember?"

"Sure. We were in two 'no' played from the North side, making."

"Oh, right. Gumpers led the ten of diamonds and you played it around to your..."

"DIRECTOR!" It was the wrathful bass of Obadiah Crawley.

A bedraggled Edmund Gradys raised himself from his chair, as he had been compelled to do so many times that night, and drew his ever-ready rulebook from its holster. "What is it?" he asked wearily. "What'd she do now?"

"I didn't do a dang thing!" cried Sally. "Nothing. Shoot, nobody's even bid yet. And it's not my turn anyhow, so you can't say I'm hesitating or holding up the game. And you can't say I'm..."

140

"Relax, dear," said Crawley, "relax. It's your teammates' behavior I'm objecting to." And he turned his cold stare on Reginald and me.

"Just what would you consider adequate compensation," Diggery inquired rather acidly, "for the frightful inconvenience caused you by the whispering of Mr. Graves and Mr. Kane? Ten, perhaps fifteen IMPs?"

"All right, all right," said Gradys, "let's try to conduct ourselves with decorum, shall we, gentlemen? After all, there's only one board to go. Play will continue and the gallery will be silent."

"One notrump," barked Buttergut almost immediately.

"Three 'no'," answered Crawley just as briskly, once Piper had passed.

And when Diggery placed the spade five on the table, I could see we were through; that this last of the Major's kamikaze tactics promised to carry the day. He'd wrestled a notrump opening out of a mangy fifteen-point holding containing no five-card suit, bullied his partner into raising to a substandard game contract, then inherited a lead and layout that would surely allow him to prevail. The first of the defense's two threats had evaporated when Diggery failed to hit on a heart lead. The second, Buttergut himself now neutralized by tricking Sally out of shifting to that same lethal suit. (Not that leading away from Kings has ever been a McGonigle trademark.) When Parker dropped his King of spades under her Ace at trick one, she had all she could do not to squeal with excitement as she tabled another spade. Euphoria gave way to dejection once Buttergut's Queen took her seven.

Parker now set about establishing the long clubs. Four of them would give him his contract; three plus the Queen of hearts or the Jack of diamonds would do the same. He finessed the club ten at trick three and was, I'm sure, somewhat disheartened when this lost to the Queen. But he did not know how safe he was, for Sally had no spade left with which to establish Diggery's suit, and had already surrendered the timing on the hand. Here was the setup:

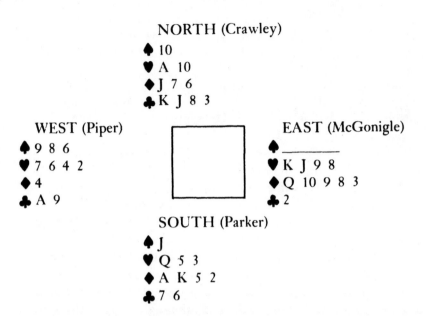

NORTH (Crawley)
♠ 10
♥ A 10
♦ J 7 6
♣ K J 8 3

WEST (Piper)
♠ 9 8 6
♥ 7 6 4 2
♦ 4
♣ A 9

EAST (McGonigle)
♠ _____
♥ K J 9 8
♦ Q 10 9 8 3
♣ 2

SOUTH (Parker)
♠ J
♥ Q 5 3
♦ A K 5 2
♣ 7 6

Three clubs would come in, Parker would pick up an extra red suit winner, and the game, match and title would go not to the Quartet but to the Caucus. And as if to second that opinion, the Major began stroking his tummy.

Yet just as Sally detached her three of diamonds with a view toward launching an attack on that suit, she suddenly drew in a deep breath, clutched her intended lead to her breast, and sneezed. Now this was no delicate drawing room ah-choo but an honest, body-wrenching, North Oklahoman honker that bedewed Hermione's outer feathers and sent a single card flying from McGonigle's left hand. High above the tabletop that wayward card sòared, until it landed face up and revealed itself to players and audience alike as his nibs, the King of hearts.

"Whoops!" cried Sally. "Touch of hay fever, I guess. Here, I'd better put that critter right back where he belongs..."

"Fat chance," growled Crawley, "and *Gesundheit*. I'm afraid where 'that critter' belongs is right where he's lying."

"Nonsense," objected Parker as he flashed an unctuous smile and suspended his right hand in mid-rub. "What are we, savages? What is this, some sort of blood game? Look here, Obadiah, the lady couldn't help her sneeze, could she? So how can I, in good conscience, hold her responsible?" I was quite taken with the Major's magnanimity. How often is one offered the head of a King on a platter?

"I can't say that I agree with you," Diggery exclaimed, quickly falling heir to the look of contempt that Sally had until then been training on Crawley. "Your generosity and sense of fair play are exemplary, of course, but as your partner has pointed out on more than one occasion this evening, a rule is, after all, a rule. We can only hope that next time Miss Sally will exercise a greater measure of control."

"No, no, no," purred Buttergut. "No, I insist that Miss McGonigle be allowed to..."

"DIRECTOR!"

"Coming, coming," mumbled Gradys as he hustled once more toward the table. "I saw what happened, Congressman."

"Then you're prepared to make a ruling?"

"You bet I am," Gradys replied with more than a hint of vindictiveness. "As dummy, you are not permitted to appeal to the director during the play of the hand. In so doing, you forfeit your team's rights to relief."

"What? You mean to tell me..."

"Tough break, Obadiah," Parker commiserated.

"Oh come, come, now," Piper protested. "Miss Sally and I waive our rights, in turn. Far be it from us to take unfair advantage of a petty technicality."

"Well," said Crawley with a look of genuine surprise, "that's sporting of you, sir. Real sporting of you." (The Chairman's bullying effusiveness made it clear to all that no further objections from Parker or McGonigle would prevail.) "Now, Gradys how about that ruling?"

"All right, all right," said the disgruntled director, who then raised aloft his collection of laws, like Moses on the mountain, and intoned: "According to Chapter Six, Part Three, Section Two, Law 58, Article B1 of *The Laws of Duplicate Contract Bridge*, 'If a defender leads or plays two or more cards simultaneously, and if only one such card is visible, he must play that card.'"

"The King of hearts is visible, the other card is not," Piper summarized as Crawley vigorously nodded in agreement. "I'm afraid that settles the issue in the Congressman's favor. Thank you, Mr. Gradys."

"Wait!" said Crawley. "I want you to stay put for the rest of this hand, just to make sure our rights are protected."

"Shoot," Sally groused, "you've got my partner here for that."

But once everyone's attention finally returned to the play of the hand, the only sound to be heard in the room was Buttergut's quiet, compulsive chanting. "Hut, two, three, four... Hut, two, three, four..." he muttered. It was then that the onlookers finally began to realize what he and Diggery had perceived from the start—that the heart King was a poisoned offering which, once accepted, would remove the only side entry to the as yet unestablished clubs; that a hold-up of the club Ace would now render that critical suit useless; that a single trick in one suit was being exchanged for three in another.

In no time at all I was able to identify this rare entry-killing sacrifice of an unsupported honor. I'd read a thorough analysis of the play some four months earlier in the silver anniversary issue of the *Icelandic Review of Bridge*. Sally McGonigle, by mistakenly tabling the one card that could possibly defeat the contract at that point in the hand, had executed what is known in expert circles as the Merrimac Coup. I felt reasonably sure, however, that this was the first instance of that arcane maneuver's resulting from an allergy to ragweed.

"HUT, two, three, four. HUT, two, three, four. HUT, two..."

"What's the problem, Winthrop?" asked Crawley in response to his partner's delay. But Parker went on marking that senseless cadence and only emerged from his near catatonia when cautioned by Gradys. Fully aware that ducking would only postpone the inevitable, Buttergut took the King with his Ace and clung to the faint hope that the Queen of diamonds would fall doubleton and permit him to reach dummy via the Jack. But this was not to be. Piper allowed one club to win, took his Ace at trick six and shot back a spade. And when the Major found the diamonds stacked

144

unfavorably to his right, he went down two.

That deal earned us eight IMPs and the match, but one would never have guessed it from listening to the words of the woman who had proved yet again that rationality and free will are by no means necessary prerequisites of heroism. "Now what on earth're you pouting about?" Sally grilled Parker. "Just remember, if they hadn't gone and made me give up my King of hearts, you'd've been minus 300 instead of 200."

At first Buttergut just sat there, apparently not having heard this deft post-mortem analysis. Then he said to the Captain, "I hope, sir, that this will not be the last time you and I meet in combat."

"If indeed it is not," Diggery replied, "I expect that next time you may pay more heed to the lessons of your country's military history."

"How's that?"

"Why, you should never have permitted the director to intervene in that final hand. Surely you recall what happened the last time a Merrimac was monitored."

Episode XII

In Which the Captain Sails from Scylla to Charybdis...
(August 2, 1983)

I have read Sailland's description of the grand hotels of the city of light and could no doubt make my way blindfolded through the halls of the Paris Ritz or the Montpensier. I know all that Sir Compton Mackenzie has to say about the Savoy; every tribute Jackson, Nicol and Contarini have paid to that same exquisite establishment. And I could recite by heart the paeans sung by Inglis to the Gritti Palace with its centuries-old masonry and facing canals. Believe me, if I ever have the time and money to travel to Paris, London or Venice, those are surely the hotels where I hope to stay. But I will always be haunted by the knowledge that I could be doing better. For in all God's earth, there can be no place, *no* place, like the Plaza.

No place anything like that marvelous institution with its surrey-ringed entranceway, its Hardenbergh facade, its blazing chandeliers, its five great marble staircases, its porters draped with sterling-silver whistles and brocade. One walks differently into the Plaza than one would, I suspect, into any other building in the world. With the bemused half-smile and sprightly step that come with having truly arrived. And it was with just such an air that the Piper Quartet entered the hotel's stately lobby on the

146

evening of August 1. There a marble fountain gently plashed and fresh-cut flowers infused the air with piquant fragrances of the summer season as we contemplated the wealth of options that lay before us. I say "we" but in truth I mean "I," for although Piper, Graves and McGonigle all claimed to have stayed at the Plaza on various occasions in the past, I knew they could not have learned a tenth as much about that magnificent edifice in one hundred visits as I had absorbed by reading and rereading everything from the collected adventures of Eloise—Kay Thompson's six-year-old in- habitant of the Plaza's top floor—to that classic source book, *The Plaza: Its Life and Times.* There was nothing about the hotel's seventy-five-year tradition of elegant (its bourgeois detractors would say decadent) hospitality with which I was unacquainted. Not the size of its staffs and operating costs over the past seven decades; not the history and scope of its interior renovations; not the wonders of its culinary offerings, as immortalized in Eve Brown's *The Plaza Cookbook.*

And so before we even ascended to our suite I insisted on treating my teammates to a tour. I chose first to lead a casual stroll around the perimeter of the famous Palm Court, where sunglassed celebrities were snifting post-prandial liqueurs, as a black-tie duo performed Chaminade sonatas for piano and flute. At the center of that hallowed enclosure I was able to identify (thanks to my total recall of all back issues of *People Magazine*) Bianca Jagger's third hairdresser and the former owner of a nightspot called Studio 54, a popular discotheque back in the seventies. Next we enjoyed a cocktail in the understated elegance of the Edwardian Room, window-shopped the extravagant boutiques that line the halls connecting the Court with the Oyster Bar, then took a light supper at the latter eatery. It was oysters Florentine and Meur- sault all around. Each portion of bubbling bivalves was served on the finest of hammered pewter, and the wine arrived chilled, as I had requested, to forty-nine degrees. I could tell that even Diggery was impressed.

"Gosh," said Sally, once we'd finished our meal, "I'm bushed."

"Yes," Diggery concurred, "perhaps we should all get a good night's rest before tomorrow's match."

"But wait," I pleaded. "We haven't seen half of what I wanted to show you. There's the walk-through tour of the kitchen and grand ballroom, the review of the wine cellar, the..."

"Maybe," Reginald broke in, "we could see all that another time..."

"Look, I'll offer a compromise. I'll skip the kitchen and ball-room and wine cellar if you'll stick with the rest of the program, all right? Now please follow me." I then led them to certain little-known hallways on the third, seventh and eleventh floors and pointed out the very suites where Congressman Pasquale Gilberto had maintained a harem of mistresses prior to his conviction for misappropriation of public funds in the winter of '79. (Here I drew heavily on kernels of information gleaned from my collection of erotic guidebooks—in particular, *Midtown on $100 a Night* by Mimi La Fong, and Christiana Honeywell's *Confessions of a Big Apple Tart*.) From the windows at the north end of each corridor, we would look out over Manhattan, now concentrating on the sparkling sea of lights along the east and west shores of the island, now dwelling upon the vast black oblong to the north that was Central Park at night.

Finally I suggested we have a nightcap in the Palm Court, where our match was due to be played at 11:00 o'clock the next morning. And lucky for us we made it back when we did. For who should have arrived just then for a midnight cup of coffee but that indefatigable mayoral candidate, Alba Belzug, resplendent in a green suede picture hat with an ostrich feather attached. I made a beeline for her table, expressed my sincere regrets that her 1981 write-in campaign had fared so poorly and wished her luck with her recently announced plans for '85.

By the time I returned to my table with her autograph, I noted that Sally, Reginald and the Captain had apparently retired to their rooms, for only the check remained. I sat back and ordered another snifter of brandy. We would be in the big city only two days, after all, and I was determined not to sleep through half of my visit. Two days, I thought. Two more days and it would all be over. The tension, the concentration, the constant feeling of being accountable to three other people. That and above all the isolation. I was sure we would lose in the morning to the New York–New England division champions (the seemingly invincible Gatch-Dublais team that had swept the Grand Nationals in each of the last four years) and that the next day I would be home in my cozy, one-bedroom Capitol Hill apartment. The morning after that I would show up bright and early at the mailroom and beg to be allowed to sort envelopes again into those beautiful brass-and-wood pigeonholes. I would say farewell to this devil's game of bridge. I would set out to win back my Jane.

How I laugh now at the innocence of those thoughts from the vantage point of my bench on this promenade. I should have known then that my fragile hopes for a return to solace and security would once again be dashed on the rocks of Diggery's cunning. (Ah, no moans, no remonstrations, dear reader, for I am giving nothing away here that was not already promised, so many hours and pages ago, in my prologue.) But shielded from this knowledge, I called for the bill—which, by 1:00 A.M., had climbed to $19.75—and paid it gladly, even throwing in a five-dollar tip. What did I care? Sure, I realized this was all too rich for my blood, and that within forty-eight hours my old routines would be as easy to slip back into as a pair of time-worn boots. But so what? At last I was where I knew, deep down, some part of me belonged. At last I was surrounded not by a class of sniggering highschoolers or a roomful of sweaty postal clerks but, how shall I say it, by the right sort of people. At last I was sipping Courvoisier at the Plaza.

At six the next morning I awoke in the throes of a horrible brandy hangover; one which took me a good four hours to dispel. The Plaza, I found, looked considerably less magical at that ungodly hour than it had the night before, so I gulped down three cups of room-service coffee and set out on a walk through Central Park. The caffeine, the exercise, the bracing dawn air, the fear of being overrun by a phalanx of grim-faced joggers—all of these factors eventually conspired to clear my head of the fuzziness and pain. By the time I rejoined my friends, I may have been taut as a coiled spring, but at least I was physically capable of playing bridge.

149

And so at 10:45 yesterday morning (Can so little time have passed between then and now?) I strutted into the Plaza's Palm Court. Since I was slightly in advance of the rest of the Quartet, I was the first to introduce myself to Matthew and Pinky DeLoe, and to their celebrated teammates, Gunther Dublais and Renata Gatch—living legends whose careers I had tracked for so many years in the seventeen bridge journals to which I subscribe. They greeted me graciously and were in no way uncivil to Sally and Reginald. But it was not long before the four of them were hovering around the Captain and stroking Hermione's long, lush tail feathers. The great Dublais himself made several flattering allusions to two of Piper's more stunning coups which had recently been written up in *Popular Bridge*, and at the same time pumped him with pointed queries intended to pierce the shield of secrecy obscuring his bridge-playing background. Needless to say, Diggery parried each thrust.

Pinky DeLoe proposed during those first few moments of pleasant banter that she and her husband play at one end of the Court against Piper and McGonigle, which left their fearsome partners to take on Reginald and me at the other. We accepted that arrangement only because it would have been awkward to do otherwise. Their strategy was obvious. They would pit their stronger pair against our weaker in the hope that their heavy artillery would so devastate our vulnerable flank that the havoc Diggery might wreak upon the soft spot in their own defense would pale by comparison.

Truth to tell, it did not greatly matter to me in which manner we were to be dispatched. I was enjoying a heady sense of fatality about the entire affair; was in fact deep in the thrall of what is referred to in the scholarly works of Rondolay Shildovik as "the Marie Antoinette Syndrome"—a slavish attention to visual detail often experienced by those unfortunates about to be ritually hanged, shot, garrotted, guillotined or otherwise disposed of by their peers. Where once there was an ornate archway leading from the Palm Court to the lobby, there was now a delicate swirl of hand-carved moldings peopled with satyrs and nymphs of lilliputian stature scandalously intertwined against a sylvan backdrop.

150

Reginald's left hand and the convention card it held were nowhere near as steady as they had appeared to be only moments before, but were now a study in infinitesimal vibration. And Diggery was no longer wearing an attractive dark vest over his blouson but rather a swatch of the densest, most tactile velour, its sheen—depending upon his movements and the resultant play of light—a subtle pastiche of four shades of violet...

... Somewhere off in the distance (Who can tell how much time had elapsed?) I heard Sally and Diggery wishing us good luck and Reginald's voice nervously trying to wake me from my reverie. But it was not before I was ushered through the scores of observers massed around our table, then seated in one of the four Queen Anne chairs, that I manged to wrench myself away from this minuscule land of escape. And only when a hefty stack of boards fell to the tabletop with a clatter, only then was I able to focus again on the larger, drabber, more threatening tableau of reality.

Graves and I quite simply did not belong in the same room with our opponents. As for the social amenities, Gatch and Dublais were friendly, witty, even charming. But when it came to bridge, they metamorphosed into single-minded agents of destruction. Within minutes we felt like some soft-bellied fish among piranhas. Throughout that entire fifty-six-board match they were unmerciful, never managing to swallow us whole (thanks to the relatively undramatic nature of the great majority of deals), but nibbling away two IMPs here, three IMPs there with voracious declarer play and razor-toothed defense until there seemed to be nothing left of us but a gleaming white skeleton. I knew that even if Piper was somehow keeping our team within ten to fifteen IMPs at the other table (to which a good three quarters of the audience had by now gravitated), we would still need a monster of a swing board at the finish to overcome such a deficit.

But then disaster struck. At long last that Damoclean sword, poised above us since January, fell upon our heads with a vengeance. Consider, if you will, the following deal:

151

NORTH (Gatch/McGonigle)
♠ A K Q 2
♥ 9 3
♦ 10 7 3 2
♣ 8 7 6

WEST (Kane/DeLoe)
♠ J 9 8 6 5 4
♥ 8 7
♦ Q
♣ J 10 9 3

EAST (Graves/DeLoe)
♠ 10 7 3
♥ 10 5 4 2
♦ J 9 8 5
♣ Q 4

SOUTH (Dublais/Piper)
♠ _____
♥ A K Q J 6
♦ A K 6 4
♣ A K 5 2

Neither side vulnerable.

WEST	NORTH	EAST	SOUTH
Pass	Pass	Pass	2 ♣ *
Pass	2 ♠	Pass	3 ♥
Pass	4 ♦	Pass	4 ♥
Pass	Pass	Pass	

* Strong and artificial.

How many pairs, I ask you, would succeed in avoiding all three seemingly odds-on slams? North/South is blessed with every Ace and King in the deck, excellent hearts and diamonds for purposes of a suit contract, and a dozen top tricks in notrump but for one sticky problem: a lack of transportation to the three spade tricks in dummy. But wouldn't you know that Gunther Dublais, surely one of the most imaginative and prolific of living bridge writers, theorists and players, was able to diagnose the terminal disease from which this holding suffered? With the knowledge that he and his partner must be holding well over thirty high card points between them, he nevertheless closed out the bidding at four hearts. And as if this were not depressing enough, I then compounded our misfortune by tabling fourth down from my longest and strongest, instantly conveying Dublais to those tantalizing spades and handing him not only a contract that might have gone down one, but a bonus of two overtricks, to boot.

Now, Renata Gatch is a princess among women. She looked at me wanly with those teal-blue eyes of hers, smiled, and cocked her head to one side in a gesture of heartfelt compassion. Losing to a player of such class somehow softens the blow.

"I guess I should've led something else," I said. "I'll bet your teammates don't lead a spade."

"You never can tell," she consoled me, but I knew she agreed with what I'd said.

"You know what's going to happen at Piper's table as well as I do," Reginald lamented once we were alone. "There's no way in the world he's going to pull up short of slam with those tickets. And even if he did, there wouldn't be the giant swing we need."

The realization that we had finally lost washed over me like a shower of warm, soothing water. I felt that strange mixture of exhilaration and relief that the novice rider experiences after dismounting, safe and sound, from his first gallop. And yet there was the inevitable disappointment of defeat. It had, after all, been a glamorous seven months. I'd learned to think of myself not as a failed instructor of literature and composition, not as a political aide *manqué*, not as a frustrated mailroom clerk, but as an integral component of a fearsome bridge machine. As a member of the Piper Quartet, I thought too of how crestfallen my teammates would be by the fact that our mission would have to be aborted. The pain was already showing in Reginald's face. A pain which, to a limited extent, I shared.

And when we trekked to the opposite end of the Palm Court in order to compare scores, my suspicions were soon confirmed. Sally appeared chipper as usual and was chatting gaily with the large crowd of kibitzers who pressed about the Quartet's home table in the hope of getting an early reading on the final results. Diggery, however, looked as glum as we did. When I asked him what happened on board fifty-six, he shook his head and replied,

153

"I suggest we tally up the rest of the scores first."

That part of the story read just about the way I thought it would. Piper had combined sparkling play with a few calculated gambles to counteract the errorless performance of Dublais and Gatch on the one hand and, let us be candid, to neutralize the "drag effect" of his own three teammates on the other. As a result we were only nine IMPs behind after the first fifty-five boards. We needed a net gain of at least four hundred thirty points on the last deal to win.

"Now, what about the final board?" the Captain asked. "Did they manage to stay out of slam?"

"I'm afraid they did," I replied.

"Hmm, I thought they might. The true expert will know to hold back. What was the contract?"

"Dublais played it in four hearts."

"And?"

I could barely hear for the ruckus being caused by the onlookers who, the instant they learned that our opponents had succeeded in stopping at the four level, began running about and shouting with excitement. I felt a violent rush of resentment. Why couldn't they wait until they were out of our presence before carrying on like that? It struck me as the crassest form of casket-dancing. "I let him make it," I confessed. "It was all my fault."

"Balderdash! A player of Mr. Dublais's ability hardly has to depend on..."

"I led a spade."

"...I see."

"You and Sally bid slam, didn't you?" Reginald asked him.

"Yes, I must admit we did."

"Were you in six hearts?"

"No, but would that I had been."

"What do you mean?" I challenged. "It's unmakable."

Diggery slowly shook his head from side to side. "After winning the club lead, which is all but automatic here—no offense intended, Terence—I would have collected trumps before testing the diamonds with my Ace. Once the Queen fell on my left, I would have counted Mr. DeLoe, my East opponent, for eight

154

cards in the red suits and prayed that, of the five remaining cards in his original holding, no more than two were clubs. I would then have proceeded to cash my club King, lead my four of diamonds and play low—not the ten, mind you—in dummy, thereby gutting his suit. The situation would now look like this (and he sketched out the following position on the starched surface of the handkerchief that always peeked from the underside of his left shirtcuff):

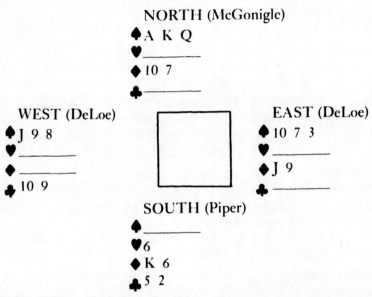

NORTH (McGonigle)
♠ A K Q
♥ _____
♦ 10 7
♣ _____

WEST (DeLoe)
♠ J 9 8
♥ _____
♦ _____
♣ 10 9

EAST (DeLoe)
♠ 10 7 3
♥ _____
♦ J 9
♣ _____

SOUTH (Piper)
♠ _____
♥ 6
♦ K 6
♣ 5 2

East would be forced to usher me to the spades in dummy one way or another."

"And if you play out your last heart winner before conceding the diamond..." Reginald began.

"I squeeze myself out of the contract," Piper concluded.

"That's ingenious!"

"Ingenious," I echoed in obvious bad humor, "but academic." Once again the flame of ambivalence was flickering bright. To hear how close we had come to victory rekindled my smoldering passion for glory and fame. Made me question the value of my newfound peace. "If not six hearts, what were you in? Six no trump?"

155

"No," he said once again, "but would that I had been. For it plays exactly the same way. You'll notice I never had to ruff anything to make the heart slam."

"He was in six diamonds," Sally offered. "And I was the one who put him there."

"That's true," said Piper, "but it matters little who was to blame."

"You mean Diggery wanted to stay below slam level," I said directly to Sally, "but you wouldn't let him?"

"He sure enough did and I sure enough wouldn't. He tried to stop at four hearts, just like Mr. Dublais. And per usual, after the bidding was good and over he came out with some of that double talk of his about duplication of values and communication problems or what not. But it's pretty darn easy to say those things after you can see both hands. It's not that simple when you're bidding, you know. Well, I looked at my two dinky ol' hearts and said, 'Uh-uh, no thanks, let's git on back to diamonds.' See, I had four of those babies and the Captain'd already bid 'em."

"Six diamonds would have given us the match," I moaned, "but there's no way to make it. Not even with the throw-in that works in six hearts and six notrump."

"Oh, I wouldn't go so far as to say that," said Diggery, flashing one of his mischievous grins. But just as he cleared his throat and prepared to spring the remainder of his surprise, a grizzled old hunchback in a linty beret stepped forward from the crowd. Suddenly Piper's face turned pale.

"*Pardon*, good sir, but you will perhaps allow an admiring bystander to inform your associates of the excellent tidings?" I cannot even now give an accurate accounting of all the violent emotions that were coursing through my breast. Who was this strange man? Why did his presence seem to have such a powerful effect on the Captain (and, as I will later explain, on me)? Had we actually defeated the Dublais-Gatch team? Were we on our way to the West Coast and a playoff with the other seven Grand National zonal champions? Was I destined to live another month in exile?

Although the gentleman remained standing, he rose only

slightly higher than the seated figure of Sally McGonigle, who smiled at him with radiant goodwill. "You go right ahead and explain, darling. The Captain won't mind somebody else tootin' that horn of his for a change." And she giggled at her gibe.

But Diggery was not laughing. He sat perfectly still and stared, quite impolitely, I thought, at the intruder's unfortunate appearance. At the grossly humped back, the grainy, meat-colored blotches marring the skin of his hands, the face so pudgy and wrinkled that there were slits where there should have been eyes, the snaggle-toothed grin with which he punctuated every phrase, and the wild white tendrils of hair that sprouted from beneath his cap in every direction, giving the impression that he lived in a never-ending state of electrical shock.

"*Eh bien*, I will proceed, then," the man said, bowing first toward Sally with a certain stiff, Old World charm. "With your permission, *mademoiselle.*"

Mais oui, monsieur, certainement!" Sally, having thoroughly mangled this humble phrase, beamed at the rest of us with a prideful glow. I should admit here that at first I had my doubts about the stooped man's French as well. My guess was that he was of Middle Eastern extraction. Lebanese, Syrian, I could not be sure. But believe me, his accent was a far cry from that of Armand Beaupère, whose argentine tones grace the monthly lessons I've been receiving in the mail now for the past six years. (I refer of course to that highly instructive series of cassettes entitled: *Your Lifelong Living Language Lab*.)

"I must begin," the mystery man continued, "by saying I have seldom witnessed a hand that was played so...so..."

"Well?" Sally ventured.

"*Ah, merci, mademoiselle, c'est le mot juste!* ...played so well. Now, Captain Peeper..." (Whether out of ignorance or an honest phonetic confusion, he pronounced the 'i' of Piper not in the Anglo-Saxon but the Gallic manner) "...received the Jack of, *comment dit-on*, clubs as a lead, the which he captured with his Ace..." I noticed that as the man spun his tale he shunned the rest of us and concentrated exclusively on Diggery, who was now staring sullenly at the carpet and pawing with one boot at its dense

157

ocher nap. "... When the Ace of trumps brings down the Queen *à gauche*, he must to himself say, this Peeper, 'I will find the other four *à droite*.' *Donc*, he essays, how do you say, tests the hearts. When West has no more the third time they are played and cannot trump, then our friend knows that East must needs have begun with four apiece of diamonds and hearts. But he does not make the great *gaffe* of cutting the third heart in his dummy..."

"Not 'cutting,'" I corrected, "'ruffing,'" In lesson fifty-seven Monsieur Beaupère explains that the French word for trumping is "*couper*," so I knew immediately what he meant. By now I was beginning to rethink my original assumption. Even if this character was of Lebanese or Syrian extraction, French might have been his native tongue after all.

"Yes, 'ruffing,' *je vous en remerci, monsieur*. You see, he must be patient, he must... denude the East hand of hearts by ruffing precisely the fourth of his own so as to create a friendly, a... a favorable situation for later on. *Vous comprenez? Alors*, Peeper plays his King of clubs so that East is made void. Then he ruffs the heart *numéro quatre* and is safe up in dummy with the spades he covets so. *Pas mal, eh?* Now the spades, they go bang, bang, bang like three bullets, and to those tricks, East must follow while *notre héros écarte*..."

"Sluffs," I tossed off nonchalantly, trying to conceal behind the veil of my linguistic expertise the difficulty I was having following Piper's intricate line of play.

"... Yes, he sluffs all that is not trumps. So now 'the table is set,' as we say in my country. If I may presume, *monsieur*." And here he scribbled out this end position on the reverse side of Diggery's handkerchief and laid it in the middle of the table:

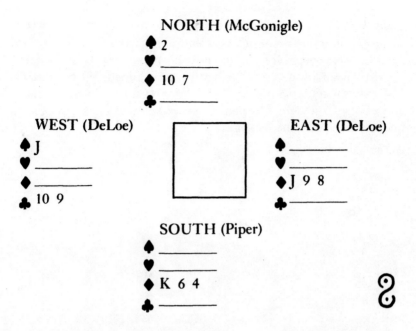

NORTH (McGonigle)
♠ 2
♥ _____
♦ 10 7
♣ _____

WEST (DeLoe)
♠ J
♥ _____
♦ _____
♣ 10 9

EAST (DeLoe)
♠ _____
♥ _____
♦ J 9 8
♣ _____

SOUTH (Piper)
♠ _____
♥ _____
♦ K 6 4
♣ _____

Do not ask me what the symbol in the lower right-hand corner was supposed to signify, but once the man had sketched it, he looked straight at Diggery and bared a gruesome collection of smoky-gray teeth.

"...And now comes the masterstroke, so elegant in its *simplicité*. *Monsieur le Capitaine* calls for the lowly two of spades, and when East plays a trump perforce..."

"Peeper underruffs!" I shouted, seeing for the first time that the hand could indeed be made.

"*Précisément.*"

"Bravo! Bravo!" I cried in way of congratulations to Diggery, who was still unaccountably enshrouded in gloom and who would not look up or make any movement, save to slip the ink-stained handkerchief back into his sleeve. "Do you see, do you see?" I asked Sally and Reginald, explaining that whoever captures the fateful eleventh trick meets death by finesse at the twelfth. This done, I turned to thank the old man, on behalf of our team, for his stirring report. But as if this were the final scene in some Lone

159

Ranger episode, the stranger had already disappeared. "Where'd he go?" I asked. "We don't even know his name."

"There is no need for you to know his name," said the Captain. "All you need know is that the battle is now joined. We have made our first contact with the enemy." Piper then rose from his chair and excused himself. His gait as he walked away was unsteady, his face an ashen shade of gray.

Epilogue

If you think I was able to wrangle even one clue from Reginald or Sally as to the identity of this man, this humpbacked kibitzer with the Levantine French whose adulatory words and sycophantic stare were enough to drive Piper from the Palm Court in confusion, you are mistaken. The two of them kept silent on that score all afternoon and throughout last night's victory celebration at Mamma Leone's. To this hour I've heard nothing on the subject other than the Captain's terse warning.

This much I can tell you, however. There was something about that man that triggered in me a sensation of *déjà vu*. Something about his diminutive stature, the curvature of his back, the almost palpably sinister force of his presence. There were times during his account of Piper's wizardry when I actually experienced tremors, so compelling was the suspicion that I had drifted before within his sphere of influence. Nor was that feeling any stronger than a premonition I now have that I will encounter him again in San Francisco.

With good reason have I spared you an account of the Quartet's bacchanalian victory feast. We were all well into our cups by the time the antipasto was served, and precious little conversation made any sense—Piper's least of all. His third goblet of Chianti seemed to usher him directly from the depression caused by his confrontation with the hunchback to a manic state of loquaciousness. Three times he began to babble about pips and dots, and three times Sally, of all people, silenced him. At midnight, in fact, she and Reginald took it upon themselves to whisk him away to our suite at the Plaza. I took that occasion to sneak off, and have been composing this journal ever since.

But now the squat saffron sun dips among the skyscrapers of Manhattan and, like a lucky balloon, descends unscathed between two steel spires. As it blends into the distant haze, I gather together my refuse of dixie cups, cellophane wrappers and dried-out pens, and rummage through my pockets for my plane ticket and cabfare. A feeling of relief overwhelms me. Through the simple expedient of committing my woes to paper, I find I have exorcised the demons of loneliness and despair. I realize, too, what a threat this document would be to the success of Operation Endplay, were it to fall into enemy hands. And so I resign myself to the fact that I dare not keep it by me, even as a silent companion, nor run the risk of sending it to Jane as an explanation, if not a justification, of my behavior. No, now that it has served its purpose, this journal must be destroyed. I cannot bear to burn these pages, but will dump them, along with my garbage, in the nearby litter basket where I have seen old cronies with shopping bags fish for discarded magazines. At least in that way the inspired bridge exploits of Captain Diggery Piper, the bumbling brilliance of Sally McGonigle, the discipline and long-sufferance of Reginald Graves—to say nothing of my own uncommon courage in the face of a bizarre fate—may bring an hour or two of solace to some tortured soul in this godforsaken city of New York.

Terence Daniel Kane
Brooklyn Heights
August 3, 1983

162

Part Three

THE FLIGHT TO
SAN FRANCISCO

It was true, thought Solomon Feinglass. He was getting careless with age. There had been a time when whatever the nature of the breakthrough or setback, he would not have shown a trace of emotion. It was a discipline in which he had been schooled by his very first supervisor back in the late forties. An art he had gone on to master and refine in the course of his long career. And not the only art. Few special agents in the Bureau's history had shown as much natural genius for surveillance and detection or demonstrated as comprehensive a grasp of the laws and procedures involved in the control of organized crime, hijacking, domestic terrorism and espionage. For thirty-seven years he had operated at the cutting edge of his awesome capabilities. And with great success. There were some who had amassed a greater number of arrests than he had (Feinglass would never rush a case and often refused to employ electronic surveillance techniques, which, he claimed, resulted in as many acquittals as convictions), but none whose intelligence, memory, intuition, stamina or attention to detail were more respected by rookies and veterans alike. It was common practice now for upcoming agents to emulate those qualities. Those and, above all, his ability to mask his emotions in

165

every professional situation. To give nothing away when investigating or interrogating, when spying or when being spied upon. To maintain at all times an inscrutable demeanor.

Yet it was this very power that now failed him. His feet—which only barely reached the floor of the Air Force transport cruising at 36,000 feet over Boulder, Colorado—cut a little jig beneath his seat as he passed the final page of the journal across the aisle. His lined, puffy face, so unaccustomed to betraying anything but the unfortunate expression he had been plagued with from birth, was now creased by a jack-o'-lantern grin, three faded-gray teeth showing gruesomely among the white. The eyes were all but hidden, as ever, behind drooping lids and the swollen flesh of his cheeks, but the slits had changed in attitude from horizontal to diagonal—an effect reminiscent of the Oriental caricature produced by children pressing templeward with their thumbs. Even when he tried in vain to settle his plump little body into a position conducive to meditation (what he had read would require sifting, analysis, dissection), and even when his back began to cause him all the usual problems, he still could not contain his satisfaction and mirth.

"You think this is funny, sir? I don't think this is funny. I don't think this is very funny at all."

"What can I tell you, Tulliver? I think it's funny."

"Oh, you do?"

"Yes, I do. You should sue me. But instead, why don't you read quietly like Croft over there. You see how hard she works? How she's not always pestering me with questions? You could learn a lot from her. Finish the document, Tulliver, then tell me if you can't find anything to smile at." Of course he would not. A well-meaning lad, Jonathan Tulliver, and as diligent a worker as he had ever had under his charge. A compulsive notetaker, a tireless searcher of records and files, a man with an unquenchable thirst for surveillance. (Wasn't it Tulliver, after all, who had tracked Kane to the promenade in Brooklyn Heights and sat patiently behind an elm for seventeen hours? Wasn't it Tulliver, and not he or the promising Deborah Croft, who had gotten this case off dead center by fishing the diary out of a trashcan?) But if

166

the man had a nose for the routine mechanics of basic police work, he lacked creativity, flexibility and, more than anything else, a sense of humor. He was rigid, at times even dense. At times almost as dense as the man whose journal he was now reading.

And what about the journal? What about the part that was not funny? It did not amuse him, after all, to be toyed with once again by his nemesis. Thanks to the diary, he had more to go on this time, but he would still have to work out what was true and what was false. Had "Diggery Piper" blundered by letting his dupe off the leash for a night? Had he really gotten drunk? Was intemperance the one chink in his armor or just another subterfuge, another feint for his adversary's benefit and for Kane's? And what was this Terence Kane being saved for? This amateur spy described by friends and relatives and landlords and colleagues and employers and girlfriends alike as "quiet," "well-behaved," "nice, but sort of dull." What role were they cultivating poor Kane to play in the grand finale? Did he deserve all the attention he was now getting? Or was he one more red herring, soon to be left floating in that bogus sea captain's wake?

"That settles it," said Tulliver as he passed the epilogue on to Croft. "With your permission, sir, while we're refueling in San Francisco, I'm going to cable the British Sail Training Academy and find out just why this Piper guy..."

"I wouldn't bother, Jonathan," said Deborah Croft. "They won't know who you're talking about."

"They won't? How do you know?"

"Sir, why didn't you tell us who we were dealing with?" she asked, fixing Feinglass with a pained look of betrayal.

"Ah, then you know?"

She held up the page containing the cryptic symbol that had been traced on the handkerchief. "This backward, dotted 'S,'" she said. "I've run across it twice now in background research. It's the trademark of a man the CIA and headquarters have given the code name 'The Gamesman.'"

"What?" cried Tulliver.

"First observed at the 1978 World Backgammon Championships in Bonn, I think it was, then two years later at the Interna-

167

tional Chess Open in Rouen. Suspected of trading in NATO defense secrets. Travels frequently between New York, Chicago, Paris, Brussels, Ankara and Leningrad, using a variety of disguises and aliases. Identity unknown. Nationality unknown. Professional affiliation, if any, unknown. CIA agent assigned to foreign surveillance: Robert Haskins. FBI agent assigned to domestic surveillance: Solomon Feinglass."

"Good, Croft... very good. Almost perfect." Was there no limit to this woman's potential? he thought. He approved of—was almost in awe of—all but the accusing tone.

"No way!" Tulliver blustered, his walrus mustache working furiously beneath his bulbous nose. "I read background reports too, you know, and I memorize the mug books, cover to cover. It was Frankfurt, not Bonn, and that's not the Gamesman's face."

"Things can be done to faces," Croft suggested. "But it *is* his method, isn't it? The game as cover, the accent, the outrageous clothes, the use of a dupe..."

"Ridiculous! You find dupes in the Gamesman's capers, sure, but not partners. He doesn't work with partners. He works alone."

"Maybe that's because the games he used in the past— backgammon and chess—don't call for partners. Or maybe his back-up people were just never discovered by our agents. After all, there were some pretty significant questions connected with the Rouen and Frankfurt cases that the boss and Haskins never got anyone to answer. Like, who fed the Gamesman his information about the ICBM placements in the first place? And exactly when did he pass it on? And to whom? I realize the stooges he recruited back then swore that, except for them, he worked on his own, but they probably saw about as deeply into those ruses as Kane sees into this one."

"Bull's-eye again, Croft," Feinglass said as he pulled six photographs from his briefcase and tossed them into Tulliver's lap. "What do you see there?" he asked.

"I know these. They're prints of the shots in the book." Tulliver picked out one tagged "Frankfurt 1978." "I see a man with blue eyes, and we all know Piper's are brown. I see a man with a

168

high-bridged nose, and we all know Piper's is straight. I see a man with a full beard..."

"Before you go any further, my friend, would you say that the man in the Rouen photos is the same as the man in the one you're looking at now?"

"Definitely. See, you can tell right here by the shape of the..."

"Fine. Now describe the facial features in the Rouen close-up."

"Let's see. Uh huh... I'd still say the eyes were blue, but... well, I guess there're a lot of yellow flecks in the first one that don't show up here."

"Tinted contacts. An old trick. And what about the nose?"

"It's not as... You know, you can't really tell much here because of the angle."

"Then try that one over there."

"Right. That's clearer. A lot clearer."

"And the bridge?"

"Well, I guess it's not as high as the other one."

"Plastic surgery, you think? Now tell me if you see any familiar faces in the background of this one. There, for example, just behind and to the left of the chess table."

"Criminy, it's her!"

"McGonigle?" Croft asked.

"No doubt about it. Would you believe it? See, the hair's black instead of auburn and she's made up to look older, but it's her all right. The same, I don't know, slow look around the mouth and eyes."

"I wonder about that," said Croft.

"Are you serious? Here, check out the cheekbones and..."

"No, I mean about her being 'slow.' I just don't buy the dumb act."

"You're kidding. You've got to be. Look, forget about the way she single-handedly blew everyone's cover. Let's just concentrate on the bridge for a minute. You play the game, don't you? The woman bids suits she doesn't hold, she supports artificial bids, she forgets about outstanding trumps, she sneezes cards onto the table—all of this when a single slip-up could knock her and her team right out of the tournament that's supposed to be so central to their mission."

"But she never loses, does she? None of her apparent errors ever turn out to cost the Piper Quartet a thing. Here, let's go through the hands Kane reports in his journal and I'll show you what I mean..."

Feinglass smiled inwardly as Croft methodically made her point. All night long he could listen to this woman and try to trace the workings of her mind. For half a year he had labored alone on this case before calling in reinforcements. First Tulliver, one month ago (he suspected that his own boss, Kincannon, was responsible for sending him Tulliver in place of the more quick-witted agent he had requested), then Deborah Croft, with whom he had never worked before but who came highly recommended by three of the Old Guard—that ever-dwindling handful of fellow agents whose methods and opinions he trusted implicitly. And as usual, they had not misled him. For after only two weeks on the case, Croft was arriving at the same conclusions as he was.

"Okay, so she lucked out again," said Tulliver. "She sneezed and the right card fell out of her hand. What can I tell you? Even this idiot, Kane, this numbskull who thinks that our boss—who's from Bayonne, right?—is some Lebanese Frenchie, even he knows it's nothing more than blind luck."

"I don't think so. I think this woman is so good a player that she can handicap her opponents and still manage to win. She might throw a partial or an insignificant game here and there just to keep up appearances, but she'll always manage to muddle through on the key hands. No, I think the flaky come-on is a pose and that she probably plays at least as well as the Gamesman himself."

"Oh, sure, and I suppose Kane is a genius too."

"No," she replied, "I expect Terence Kane is as naive as he seems. The Gamesman and his crew have been taking him for a ride from the start. First they tricked him into thinking that he'd uncovered an illicit espionage plot by dropping clue after clue under his nose until he finally picked up the false scent—the McGonigle woman's 'forgetting' that she was supposed to have been with Graves abroad, her slip of the tongue over Bahrein, the briefcase exchanges at the Capitol South metro stop and at Dupont Circle. By the way, that was you Kane was standing behind

170

at the chess game, wasn't it, sir? When he was pretending to listen to that Sister Althea Mungerson?"

"Yes. Yes, that was me. Go on."

"Wait, let me get this straight," Tulliver interrupted. "Piper knows that Kane has the Bradley Arms staked out on the very day he's to make his information drop, but it's okay with him? Oh, come on, Deb, give me a break."

"First of all, there probably wasn't any drop. Just a bunch of empty attaché cases being passed around. The Gamesman may have waited days, even weeks, for Kane to start playing sleuth before he finally spotted him across the street in Folger Park one morning and set the prearranged charade in motion. Graves, McGonigle and the Dupont Circle shills at the center chess table all had their roles to play. McGonigle's ridiculous wig, for example—like the rest of her dumb-broad image—was probably calculated to stroke Kane's ego. To make him feel that there was at least one member of this group to whom he could feel intellectually superior. Then when Kane confronted his suspects, they 'straightened him out' on the objectives of their noble mission and gave him an invitation—a command, really—to join them. They fed him the line that he knew too much not to be included in their plans, and he swallowed it whole."

Feinglass nodded his approval. "Well done so far, Croft. Yes, we seem to agree right down the line. Now maybe you can see why I didn't tell you who you were locking horns with here. You see, I wanted your opinion as to what was phony and what was real. I didn't want to prejudice the issue by warning you at the start that you were dealing with a master of deception. I wanted the benefit of your instincts. Oh, and yours too, Tulliver, naturally."

"Yeah, well, I still don't see why they'd pick someone like Kane to . . . "

"Think of it, Jonathan," Croft continued. "The man is the perfect pigeon: too susceptible to flattery, too obsessed with bridge, and too downright stupid to see that he was being lured into a web. And so when Terence Daniel Kane, a nobody in his own and in society's eyes, was asked to join an Interpol operation and was furnished with a cover that catered to his wildest fantasies of bridge superstardom, what could he do but grab at the chance? From then on his 'co-agents' basically kept him in the dark on the spy scam, just spooning him a lie or two whenever he got antsy or whenever the need arose to... to respond to outside influences."

"Outside influences?" Feinglass inquired, seeing clearly what she meant and finding the euphemism patronizing. He would flush her into the open.

"Yes, sir. The nighttime appearance in the Mercedes at the Capitol ellipse. The symbol drawn on the handkerchief during the Palm Court match at the Plaza. Excuse me for saying so, sir, but I think your intrusions into their scheme might have been a little...impulsive."

"Whereas the Gamesman's reaction was...?"

"Well, poised, I would say. Professional. He used you, sir, to give Kane the illusion of having contacted an enemy agent in the flesh."

He did not argue the point, for he had no real defense. There was a day when he could have waited indefinitely for a case to unfold, to develop its own organic rhythms and internal logic. Perhaps no more. Perhaps the pressure being applied from Washington was finally getting to him. In any case, he had intervened prematurely. Had tried to force an acceleration of pace. At the time, he'd told himself that it was to leave no question as to where both sides stood. But could there ever really have been any doubt? Surely the Gamesman had known to within a day when the monitoring had begun. Had no doubt banked on it. Nothing irked Feinglass more, in fact, than this flagrant display of *chutzpah*. It was embarrassing enough that the Gamesman had brazenly staged the first phase of his operation right in Washington, but the crowning insult was that Feinglass himself was to be included in his archenemy's design. It had by now become obvious that the role in which he had been cast would develop in part by design, in part spontaneously—Feinglass acting, the Gamesman reacting, broadening the parameters of his original conception to account for his adversary's whims, manipulating him from afar, preying on what Croft had called his impulsiveness.

He watched her now as she paused to clear her throat and adjust her eyeglasses. She looked nervous, as if she felt she had overstepped her bounds. As if she regretted the way her enthusiasm had propelled her forward.

"Excuse me, sir. I didn't mean to sound so negative."

"No, no, Deborah. There's not a thing you've said that I can object to." She blushed when he called her "Deborah." It was not a common practice for him to address his fellow agents by their first names.

Tulliver shifted in his seat. "I don't get it. If this guy really is the Gamesman—and I'm still not saying he is—then why haven't we put the arm on him and his pals? What're we waiting for, anyway?"

"They don't have the goods yet," Feinglass replied. "As of now there's not a shred of hard evidence against them. If I took what we have now back to Inspector Kincannon, he'd laugh me out of his office."

"Then all we've got to go on is this bridge freak's diary?"

"No, I've come up with a few suspects this time—Jason Struthers, Congressman Forster's legislative assistant, and Katherine Dibbs, Chief Counsel for the Senate Foreign Relations Committee. Both fraternized regularly last year with Graves and McGonigle, both have access to classified NATO defense data, and both seem to be making larger bank deposits lately than their government salaries alone could account for."

"Sounds like enough to nab *them*, at least," said Tulliver.

"Not nearly enough. And even if it were, I wouldn't touch those two until I knew for a fact that our man had the merchandise."

"But how do we know when that's going to happen?"

"In all probability," said Croft, "it will happen during the final round of the Grand Nationals event in San Francisco. During the last deal, to be exact."

"A microdot attached to one of the pips on the five of spades?"

173

asked Feinglass, half rhetorically. He found he could not stifle the urge to prove to this woman that he was with her step for step.

"Yes, sir, in all probability."

"Wait a minute," Tulliver pleaded.

"And you do well to hedge your bet, Croft, with the words 'in all probability.'"

"Yes, sir."

"Wait! Hold it!"

"After all, it's unclear, isn't it, whether or not Kane was meant all along to overhear the references to the microdot and to the pips on the five of spades? And as for the Gamesman's shock at learning that his dupe had heard more than he'd let on, who's to say whether that reaction itself was genuine or staged? There's really no way of telling, is there?"

"No, sir."

"Stop right there! I demand an explanation!"

Feinglass yawned and massaged the muscles of his neck. "Croft will give you an explanation," he said wearily. Then he turned toward the empty seat to his left and shut his eyes, as before. But this time he was preparing for sleep. . . .

"Sir? Excuse me, sir." It was Croft. At first he made as if he had not heard her. As if he had fallen asleep while she and Tulliver were talking. "Are you still awake, sir? Because there's something that still puzzles me. It's Kane's part in all this. Why do you think they need him along? And what will his role be in San Francisco? A fall guy? A carrier? A blind?"

"To answer your second question, Croft, I don't know. It's something I've been asking myself for a long time now. To answer your first question, I am still awake, yes, but I don't intend to be for long. The Nationals don't even start for another ten days. We'll talk over everything that's happened so far, analyze the journal together, line by line, I promise you. But not now, please. Now I want to rest."

For what he hoped would be the last time during that flight, Solomon Feinglass nestled his twisted back into the two pillows

174

arranged behind him and tried to induce sleep. But as always, the questions came: Whether Kane was in physical danger... Whether the Gamesman, too, had learned of the diary's existence... Whether there had been someone watching Tulliver watching Kane... Those and dozens more like them. Then the questions he had lately been finding it as difficult to ask as to answer: Whether he still had the energy for a case like this... Whether perhaps he was getting too old...

Part Four

THE FALL OF THE
HOUSE OF CARDS

"Here we go, sir, this is it. The last deal of the whole damn thing. Now we'll see."

"Quiet, Tulliver. And get back to your monitors."

"Croft and Bertrel are watching the Room A screens. There's no way you need three people to cover what's going on in there. I thought I'd give you and Collins a hand."

"Just do what you're told and stay out of my way."

Solomon Feinglass leaned forward in his chair and examined in turn the three closed-circuit monitors arrayed before him: the one to his left, showing a close-up of the cards held by the South and West competitors in Room B; the center screen, offering an overhead view of the tabletop; and the one on the right, on which the North and East holdings could be observed. As the players fanned their cards and began sorting them into suits, he did not so much as blink.

Although Feinglass and his subordinates had the six monitors virtually to themselves, they were by no means alone. Nine days before, the conference areas and futuristic twenty-two-story-high lobby of San Francisco's Hyatt Regency Hotel had been transformed into the setting for what turned out to be the largest bridge

179

tournament in the fifty-eight-year history of the game. During the ten days from August 13th to 22nd, an estimated six thousand members of the American Contract Bridge League left the comfort of their hometown duplicate clubs to compete in the individual, pair and team events of the 1983 Summer North American Championships, and—in the case of the six to seven hundred saucer-eyed enthusiasts who stayed on until the last day—to track the final-round action of the Grand National Knockout Team tournament, now winding down in one of the Hyatt's second-floor suites. Perhaps a third of that latter gathering still remained huddled in a specially cordoned-off section of the lobby to follow the last deal of what had been a painfully anticlimactic match. And of those, very few paid much attention to the six live videotape monitors, which tended to give a cramped and disjointed view of the proceedings. The majority of the audience concentrated instead on the Vu-Graph presentation, in which a panel of three experts received card distribution and bidding data from recorders located in the two closed playing areas, manually transcribed that information onto framed celluloid sheets, projected the prepared transparencies onto a fifteen-foot screen and analyzed the play as it progressed.

Feinglass tuned out the buzz of the crowd and the infuriating tongue-clucking of the woman sitting behind him, who kept registering her disapproval of the blunders made by Piper, McGonigle and Graves. He ignored the crackling of gum wrappers and the foot-shuffling of departing members of the audience too bored by the lack of suspense even to hang on for the last thirteen tricks. He heard, but no longer listened to, the uninspired commentary of the panelists who, a full hour ago, had predicted a runaway victory for the Phoenix team. All of this he blocked out while keeping his eyes fixed on the monitor to the far right, where Piper's cards and the cards of Marya Kolezar were clearly visible. For it was at the center of Kolezar's holding that he'd spotted the five of spades.

"Take Collins and Bertrel," he radioed Deborah Croft, who was sitting more than half a row away in front of the Room A monitors, "and seal off the north corridor on the second floor. I'll

180

contact you again when it happens. And it is going to happen. I can feel it."

"Yes, sir."

"Let me watch your screens, *please*," Tulliver begged.

"What are you doing here? Stay put, do you hear me? There's no one to cover for you now."

"Damn."

Once Kolezar became declarer in a one-notrump contract, the commentators explained that she held seven outright winners and no likely prospects for an overtrick, then promptly switched off their microphones, put down their wax pencils and left. Onlookers on all sides followed suit, forcing Feinglass—perhaps the shortest person in the entire audience—to stand up in order to see. He now stared more intently than ever at Piper's and Kolezar's hands as they flipped cards mechanically to the gray felt surface of the table. For a moment he thought he detected uncharacteristic signs of nervousness in the way Piper kept collapsing his holding, then spreading it out anew, then reversing the order of his suits. Yet so many things about the man were different that day. The outrageous clothes, the parrot, the sparkling play were all gone. His whole effect seemed muted, low-keyed. Now that he'd maneuvered himself into position to achieve his hidden objective, he seemed to be throwing the match and preparing an unobtrusive getaway. Though these thoughts, triggered by Piper's fretful hand movements, flitted instantaneously through his mind, Feinglass found himself losing his concentration. He refocused immediately on the image of the five of spades, cautioning himself not to be distracted by the conman's shells. To keep his eyes on the pea.

He watched Kolezar capture Sally McGonigle's opening diamond lead, run the Ace-King of hearts, then play the spade five toward dummy's Ace at trick four. There were no sudden or irregular movements on anyone's part. Declarer dropped the five atop her overturned stack of winners and moved on. Next she played out her Ace and King of clubs and cashed a third heart winner for her seventh trick. Finding that the enemy hearts were not distributed evenly, she tossed in her remaining six cards and made an open-palmed gesture of concession.

"What a bust!" said Tulliver, suddenly materializing again at Feinglass's side. "Zero, right? I mean, a big nothing. Forget the microdot business. Forget the five of spades. Sorry, boss, but for my money at least, this settles all the hooey about Piper being the Gamesman. Just an ordinary cardsharp, from the looks of it. And not too hot at that, either. I mean, Jesus, wasn't the bridge a joke? Did you believe how he mangled that four-heart hand three boards back?"

Viewers were now leaving their seats in droves and milling about, openly discussing the match. Feinglass, unable to maintain an unobstructed view of the monitors from where he stood, climbed onto his chair. From that height he saw Piper and Kolezar engaging in what appeared to be a postmortem. Soon both figures rose from the table and walked beyond the range of the room's battery of cameras.

"Look, sir, if it'll make you feel any better I'd be glad to go up there and inspect the deck they were using."

"No!" Feinglass cried, causing a momentary hush to fall over a wide area of the lobby. "I want no one to touch those cards before the Gamesman makes his move."

Tulliver looked about uneasily. "Sir? I wish you'd get down from there. Everybody's staring at us."

But then it happened. Following ten to fifteen seconds during which the Room B monitors showed nothing but the card-strewn tabletop, Piper's disembodied arm and hand suddenly knifed across the center and right-hand screens and carved out Kolezar's collection from among the others.

Feinglass flicked on his radio control. "Croft... Croft?"

"Yes, sir?"

"Take up a position at the door. No one is to leave." He scrambled down from the chair and hurled himself into the crowd, his elbows protruding before him like menacing horns, his tousled white hair whipping this way and that, his humped back heaving with effort. Once through, he bounded up the staircase to the second floor and ran as best he could down the north corridor, at the end of which he joined forces with Croft, Collins, Bertrel

182

and Tulliver, who arrived seconds later.

That raiding party of five then burst into the front hall of the playing suite, sped through the vacated Room A (where Terence Kane, Reginald Graves and pair two of the Southwest zonal championship team had lately competed), dodged past a startled gathering of Grand National officials who were computing the match's results in the central room of the suite, and threw open the door to Room B. There they came upon the tournament director and all eight contestants.

"Diggery!" Kane shouted as soon as he spotted the humpbacked figure panting furiously at the threshold. "Diggery, it's him!"

"I want you all to stay exactly where you are," Feinglass commanded.

"Who are you?" challenged the director. "What are you doing here? Do you people realize where you are?"

"We're agents of the Federal Bureau of Investigation," Feinglass announced, exhibiting his credentials for all to see as he deliberately made his way toward Piper. "The three of you known as 'Reginald Graves,' 'Sally McGonigle' and 'Captain Diggery Piper' are charged with espionage and are hereby placed under arrest. Tulliver, show them the warrants and read them their rights."

"Hey, what is this?" Kane protested over Tulliver's drone. "What are you trying to pull? Here, let me see those credentials."

"Cool it," snapped McGonigle in a drawl-free voice. "Will you cool it just for once?"

Kane recoiled from that sound as from a snake. "What the..."

"Surprised by what you hear?" asked Feinglass. As he spoke, he kept his eyes trained on Piper's hands and on the packet of cards they cupped. "You'll be escorted to the FBI Building on Golden Gate Boulevard, Mr. Kane, where we'll want to get a statement from you concerning your recent activities and the company you've been keeping of late. We'd appreciate it if you'd remain available for a routine questioning session this evening, as well, and at some point in the future you'll be expected to testify as a prosecution witness. Otherwise, you may consider yourself a free man."

183

Feinglass now took the cards from Piper's hands, at the same time extracting a white, oblong object from the inside pocket of the man's suit jacket. "What have we here, Captain? Already stamped, I see, and neatly addressed to *'Besitzer'*—that's German for 'Occupant,' isn't it?—Theaterstrasse 4, CH-8001 Zürich, Schweiz. It's empty, but it's just the right size for, oh, a playing card, say." He turned over the top card of the thirteen he held and produced the five of spades. "Like this one."

"Tell me," said Piper with a smirk, "is this one of those clever conjurer's tricks where you end up pulling a card out of someone's nose or ear?" He too now spoke without an accent.

"Diggery!" Kane exclaimed. "I don't get it. What's going on?"

"You seem to be enjoying this game of yours," said Sally McGonigle to Feinglass. "But I wish you'd explain the rules so we could all play."

"Oh, it's not my game, Miss McGonigle, or whatever your real name is. It's your partner's. And to tell you the truth, I didn't start enjoying it until about a week ago. But I do get a kick out of winning, I'll give you that. The sort of kick the Gamesman here probably got after Frankfurt and Rouen. The sort of kick he might have gotten this time, too, if he'd learned to resist playing to a crowd."

"So many riddles," said Piper. "I wish I knew what you were talking about, or what significance that card you're brandishing is supposed to have, but I don't."

"A pity," said Feinglass as he ran his index finger over the pips of the five of spades. His deadpan expression belied the emotion he was now feeling. In the end, his sense of timing had not failed him; he had sprung the trap at precisely the right moment. His patience, his painstaking methods of surveillance had been rewarded. He would be vindicated in full. "But you'll find out what's going on soon enough. In fact, I'll be sure to fill you in myself after I read the message on the microdot I expect to find hidden on the surface of this card."

Piper's smile now looked forced. "And how, if I may ask, did you come to believe you'd find this, what did you call it, this..."

"Microdot."

184

"...Thank you...this microdot on the five of spades?"

"Why, I read Mr. Kane's diary, of course."

"Mr. Kane's *what*?" cried Graves.

"My diary, Reginald. I kept a diary. But I threw it away. I don't understand how they could've known where it was. I don't understand anything about what's happening here."

"Bertrel, Collins, take them away," Feinglass ordered. "Croft, confiscate the videotape and voice recordings that were made in both rooms. Tulliver, before you take Kane in and get his statement, I want you to phone Inspector Kincannon at the Hoover Building, Robert Haskins out in Langley and Sylvia Long at Justice. Tell them they're all invited to a private screening at our Frisco headquarters tonight. Let's make it nine o'clock, California time. Arrange to have someone pick them up at the airport."

"A private screening, sir?"

"I filled them in last weekend. They'll know exactly what I mean."

"You're repeating yourself, Mr. Feinglass. I got your point about this McGonigle woman the first time you made it. You don't plan to take as long on this briefing as you did on the case, do you?"

Every physical characteristic of James Kincannon, Inspector at the FBI's national headquarters in Washington, bespoke an assertiveness verging on the hostile. His hair, hacked down to a fierce Marine crewcut by a boot-camp barber in the early fifties, had been kept ever since at regulation length. His voice, loud to begin with, was constantly being supported by a host of poking and pounding gestures. An odor of rancid oil hung on his breath and radiated from his clothes, owing to the huge supply of peanuts which he crammed into his jacket and pants pockets every Monday morning and munched throughout the week. Even the shape of the man's torso struck many of his associates as threatening. He was tall, bull-necked and compactly round. The front of his body, like a veteran stevedore's, showed no evidence of either a paunch or a waist, but instead was defined by a gradually bulging arc

185

running from the base of the neck down to the top of the legs. And from one end of that arc to the other there was nothing soft or yielding, for Kincannon was not so much fat as marbled.

United States Attorney Sylvia Long, not daring to blunt the rhetorical edge of the Inspector's question by speaking too soon, allowed his words to hang suspended for several seconds in the brightly lit screening room. Then she smiled and said, "This has all been very enlightening, Agent Feinglass. If the microdot bears out what you've said up to now, my staff and I should have an airtight case."

"A fine piece of police work, Solomon," CIA agent Robert Haskins agreed. "I don't mind telling you I feel a little envious. After all, you've succeeded brilliantly where I failed. Yes, and mark my words, putting the Gamesman out of commission will be seen as the capstone of your career."

"Oh, come on, Robert. There was more luck involved than brilliance and you know it."

"All right, all right, Mr. Feinglass, why don't you stow the false humility and wrap this thing up. I don't intend to miss TWA's Red Eye back to Washington tonight."

"Yes, sir. But as I mentioned at the start, when we inspected the microfilm negative this afternoon in the lab, we found that the message was in cipher. So what I did was contact a specialist..." Feinglass, who for the past forty minutes had held forth on the dais at the front of the auditorium, now retold the story of how he had summoned a cryptanalyst from the National Security Agency codebreaking division in Fort Meade, Maryland; of how that woman had been working on the microdot for the past hour and a half; of how the NSA computer bank could be relied upon to decipher the message if it was indeed decipherable. He was stalling for time and the process was doubly painful. For not only was he being badgered by Kincannon for dragging his feet, but he despised being the center of attention in the first place. It always made him feel self-conscious about his appearance. "...and once she breaks it, our own staff will..."

"I know, I know, Mr. Feinglass. 'Our own staff will make copies of the plain text available for everyone's perusal.' Wasn't

186

that how you put it a quarter hour ago?"

"I believe it may have been, sir, yes. Now, the problem with the cipher, as Ms. Crosley explained it to me, is that..." At that moment the door at the back of the hall opened and Feinglass breathed a sigh of relief. An angular woman of severe expression walked quickly down the center aisle. Five or six steps behind her came a man pushing a mounted microdot projector before him and struggling to keep up. "Any luck, Ms. Crosley?" Feinglass called out.

"Yes," was her reply.

"But what's the projector for? I thought the microdot was enciphered."

"The *first* microdot was enciphered," she said, her pale, thin lips barely moving as she spoke, "the second was not."

"The second?"

"The first message, attached to the center pip of the playing card you gave me, did nothing more than direct its reader to a second dot concealed not on a pip but on one of the digits."

"But why?" asked Sylvia Long. "What was the point?"

"Who knows?" said Haskins. "Probably just one more game. A bit of gallows humor on the off chance that the card might be intercepted. Even in defeat the Gamesman stays in character."

"A plausible explanation," said Crosley, "since the cipher itself took the form of a cryptological joke." This last word she pronounced drily, almost contemptuously. "It was, to be precise, a straddling bipartite monoalphabetical substitution superenciphered by modified double transposition—a variant of the virtually unbreakable system first developed by the Russians for use in this country during the 1950's. The four keys employed by the individual who enciphered the five-of-spades microdot message turned out to be the same four keys that were used on the infamous 'Vic cipher' publicized during the 1957 trial of Rudolf Ivanovich Abel. It was no more than a game of cat and mouse—in the end, rather insulting, really."

"Okay, okay," said Kincannon, "but it doesn't sound like anything you won't get over. Now how about projecting the microdot we *can* read."

Not even pausing to acknowledge this directive, Henrietta Crosley, her job done, turned on her heels and left the auditorium. Feinglass smiled, seeing an opening. "Sir, Ms. Crosley is probably the foremost authority in the country on cryptanalysis," he said with some relish, "but she's a little high-strung. I guess she doesn't see the actual projecting of the microdot onto the screen as being within her bailiwick. Anyway, we've got our own man Gervin here for that. He's been cleared, along with the four of us, to read the microfilm, sir."

"All right, all right, so who needs her?"

"Yes, sir."

"By the way, is everyone else on hand, Mr. Feinglass? Did you take care of that?"

"Yes, I did, sir. Agent Croft and two men from a local field squad have the suspects under guard in an office at the back of the hall."

"What about the witness?"

"Agent Tulliver's keeping him company in the conference room through the door to the right of the screen."

"Okay, then, let's douse those lights, son," Kincannon blared in the direction of the technician who stood waiting in the aisle, no more than ten feet away.

His ordeal at last at an end, Feinglass stepped down from the dais and slumped into the seat next to Haskins at the end of the second row. And yet it was not until the auditorium was thrown into darkness that he was able to relax completely. As he listened to Gervin's hurried footfalls leading from the light switch at the rear of the hall back to the overhead projector, he allowed himself what he was sure must have been an imperceptible smile. It occurred to him then that the anticipation of his triumph would be enough. That he might even resent its realization for putting an inalterable end to the hunt; for closing off all the trails that might still have awaited; for calcifying his investigation in time. He could imagine nothing sweeter than this savoring of what was yet to come, a sensation which reached an almost unbearable intensity at that immeasurable interval between the time when the screen before him suddenly came alive with hundreds of printed charac-

188

ters and the time when their symbolic meaning was comprehensible to the human mind. And so when Solomon Feinglass read the following words, his subsequent state of depression might in some perverse sense have been described as less than complete:

Dear Special Agent Feinglass:

Do you read mysteries for pleasure? It doesn't necessarily stand to reason that you do, you know. There are actors, or so I have heard, who will read anything but a play in their leisure time, and poets who, once they put down their pen for the evening and repair to the bookshelf, avoid all forms of verse like the plague. Are you like them, I wonder? Or are you familiar with the great mystery classics? Did you learn, for example, the lesson taught by Poe's Monsieur Dupin in The Purloined Letter—*that the safest place to conceal a coveted missive may be directly beneath the noses of those most eager to find it? And has a familiarity with the opus of Dame Christie cured you, I'm curious to know, of that all but universal habit of trusting a first-person narrator not to have committed so dastardly a crime as* The Murder of Roger Ackroyd *or, to move closer to home, the smuggling of a contraband microdot?*

My reason for asking is this: The case on which you've been laboring for lo these many months was cast, from its very inception, in the literary-mystery mold. If you understand how the masters of the genre use flawed narrators, misleading tone and mood, ambiguous dialogue and deceptive point of view to cover their acts of fictional prestidigitation, then my guess is you have me in custody at this moment. And if this is so, my employer—whom I am not at liberty to name—congratulates you. The third game, he entreats me to say, is proclaimed yours. But if I am not under wraps, if I managed to slip away before the first message was deciphered and this second one read, then I'm afraid you lose again.

There are details about this caper which must regrettably remain

"What the hell is this nonsense?" Kincannon bellowed, spewing forth a shower of nut pulp in his rage. But he received no reply, for Feinglass had already bolted from his seat and was now scuttling across the dais toward the conference-room entrance.

"Solomon!" Haskins called out. "I thought you said the Gamesman was being held in the *back* office."

When Feinglass yanked open the door, he found Jonathan Tulliver, cigarette in hand, sitting back on the hind legs of a chair and puzzling over the Ira Corn bridge column in that day's San Francisco *Chronicle*. "Where is he?" Feinglass cried.

Tulliver leaped to his feet, which until then had been resting on the long hardwood table that bisected that room. Since there were no ashtrays available (he had been flicking his ashes onto the carpet), he was now forced to hold his cigarette at his side and to look on, mortified, as a bluish-gray ribbon of smoke curled playfully between him and his superior on its way toward the vent above their heads. "You mean Kane, sir?"

"WHERE IS HE?"

Tulliver hustled to the room's one window and pointed toward Golden Gate Avenue three stories below. "He's right there in that phone booth, sir. See? The one with the light on and with the raincoat hanging from the inside door handle."

"How long has he been out of your sight?"

"Out of my sight? How do you mean out of my sight, sir?"

"How long has it been since you actually saw him last?" Feinglass's voice quavered with frustration.

"I don't know. An hour, an hour and a half...."

"What? An hour and a half?"

"Sure. See, after I took his statement, we grabbed a brew and a sandwich at the Zodiac, this place over in North Beach. Dancers and all, you know? Anyhow, we checked out a few more joints along the strip, then he starts talking about catching a plane. Okay, I remind him about hanging around for tonight's session, right? He says fine, he'll get a later flight, and in the meantime, he'll be talking to his girlfriend—you remember, boss, that Jane he wrote about in his diary. So he goes into that booth at about 8:15, I guess, with a ton of change in his pockets. Like it's going to take a while to break her down. Said to interrupt him whenever I had to."

"You idiot!"

190

"Look, I'll go get him right now if you want. No prob. Take me two minutes."

"Get on the phone and contact Chief of Police Havens, do you hear me? Tell him to put out an APB for the arrest of anyone answering Kane's description..."

"Right," said Tulliver, whipping out his pen and pad. "Hold on, let me get this down, sir."

"...Phone John Grabowski at the FAA in Washington and see if he'll authorize an hour delay in all departures from San Francisco International and Oakland Airports..."

"'San Francisco International and Oakland Airports.' Right, sir."

"...See that a car is waiting for me out front when I leave this building, which should be in ten to fifteen minutes. And then, Tulliver, then stay out of my sight for as long as you live. Do you hear me? I don't want to see you ever again."

"'Ever again.' Right, got it."

When Feinglass stormed back into the auditorium, he saw that Kincannon had not been idle in his absence.

"Let's go, let's go. I haven't got all night to waste out here."

"What are you doing, sir?" Feinglass asked as he watched Deborah Croft march Piper, McGonigle, Graves and their three lawyers down the center aisle of the auditorium, around the projector and into the front row of seats.

"Did you find your man in there, Mr. Feinglass?"

"No, sir."

"Fine, so that's about, what, a year's work wasted?"

"Unless we can nab Kane before he leaves the country."

"Uh huh. And just how much of a lead does this 'dupe' you've been telling us about have on you?"

"About an hour and a half, sir."

"Oh, great. Good luck, Mr. Feinglass. But in the meantime, I wouldn't worry about why our friends are being invited to join us."

"Friends!" cried Feinglass. "Don't you know yet who this man and his accomplices are? Just look at the photographs again or ask Haskins, if you don't believe me. Don't you see what they've done? Don't you realize they're the very ones who put Kane up to the whole..."

"Of course I do," the Inspector cut in. "What do you take me for, a dull normal? But let's be realistic, Mr. Feinglass. The fact is, you've been hoodwinked, slickered. Am I right or am I wrong?"

"...You're right, sir."

"Yes, and as for letting these birds in here now, you don't think there's any danger that they'll be reading classified NATO defense information, do you?"

"No, sir."

"No, neither do I. Well, I may have a question or two to ask them before I leave, if that's all right with you and with their lawyers."

"For sure," said the tallest and tannest of the attorneys just as Kincannon paused to grind down a fresh batch of peanuts. "Ask away." The man wore a blue Dacron suit, a white turtleneck sweater and an enormous gold medallion bearing the image of the Aztec sun god. "'Course I can tell you now there's no way you're going to link our clients with this bummed-out mail clerk you seem to be after. Hey, they were bridge buddies, sure, but if you're talking conspiracy—and I'll tell you, *amigos*, that's what I'm hearing—then..."

"Shaddap!" growled Kincannon once he'd regained the capacity to talk. "All right, let's go, kid," he called to the projectionist, who then moved a second portion of the message onto the screen:

then I'm afraid you lose again.

There are details about this caper which must regrettably remain secret. For instance, I cannot tell you what was stolen, nor from whom. On that latter score, however, you should know that my unwitting decoys, Jason Struthers and Katherine Dibbs, are guilty of nothing save perhaps failing to report for income-tax purposes the regular installments of cash I anonymously funneled them. And Piper, McGonigle and Graves—my dupes, if you will—of course know nothing. All the incriminating dialogue attributed to them in my journal was pure fiction and, for trial purposes, inadmissable hearsay, I'm sure.

192

But let's move on to a matter which, assuming I'm on the loose, can now be safely revealed. If you examine the closed-circuit coverage of the final Grand National deal in Room A, you may detect my palming of the five of spades just as I was rising to leave the table. On one of the pips of that card was hidden a microdot, as advertised: a microdot whose message would no doubt interest you far more than the one you're now reading. So you see, you came close. Right card, wrong room.

So much for method and opportunity, always rather dull consider-

"Tulliver," Feinglass muttered bitterly under his breath.

"What's that, Mr. Feinglass?"

"Nothing, sir."

"Wasn't that Kane the deceitful one!" exclaimed Piper. "Sally, Reginald, it seems certain now our teammate was some sort of spy after all."

"So we finally meet again," said Haskins with open contempt. "It's been a long time since Rouen."

"I beg your pardon, sir, but do I know you?" Piper asked, turning halfway around in his seat. "I'll admit your voice sounds familiar, but it's awfully difficult to make out faces in here."

"Oh, this is a bit much," said Sylvia Long. "It's bad enough that the four of them telegraphed every move they were going to make and still got away with it. But then to have them laugh in your face is just the limit."

"'The four of them'?" inquired Sally McGonigle, affecting once again the voice of an ingénue. "Then you're pretty sure Terry had accomplices?"

"Gosh, he must have," Graves offered. "The whole thing seems too complicated for one man to bring off alone."

"Okay, that's enough out of you two," said Kincannon. He signaled to the projectionist. "Just keep the stuff coming from now on, son, right to the end.

the one you're now reading. So you see, you came close. Right card, wrong room.

So much for method and opportunity, always rather dull consider-

ations when compared with motive, don't you agree? Then again, you already know my motive. Thanks to the background check you must have run on me at the start of this case, you've known all along that the story of my life, at least until recently, is not a jot more exciting than it was described in the prologue of my journal. You were willing to believe, weren't you, that a man who had subsisted for so many years on a diet of social, academic and professional mediocrity would snatch at the chance to participate in an espionage mission? Well, you were right. I was approached in the spring of 1982—five years after I'd clawed my way out of graduate school, two years after I'd fled Sibley High, seven months after my patron, Kevin O'Flaherty, had been incarcerated, and five months, two weeks and six days after my servile duty in the Congressional mailroom had begun. From your point of view and, I suppose, from my employer's, I was a chicken ripe for plucking. But I have not once regretted my decision.

As for the risk I ran of being caught, I stipulated at the outset that the more convoluted the game you and I were to play, the better; that the more complex the plot and the more intricate the character I would be expected to create, the more eager I would be to participate. I reasoned all along that if I were to succeed in putting across my book-bound, bridge-obsessed chump, my euphoria would know no bounds; and that if the whole thing collapsed under its own weight, I probably wouldn't find it any more boring to stamp out license plates in some federal penitentiary than to facilitate the flow of earth-shattering information between the nation's leaders and the electorate.

Farewell, Special Agent Feinglass. My last instruction was to compliment you on the quality of the chase and to ask you to convey my employer's regards to one Robert Haskins, whose turn, he wishes me to add, comes next.

Sincerely as ever,
Terence Daniel Kane

"Oh, that's swell," said Kincannon as the lights were turned back on, "just swell. And I don't suppose you know a thing about any of this, do you, Piper?"

194

"I should say not. Believe me, I'm shocked."

"How do you think *I* feel?" asked Graves. "I've known Terry longer than anyone here. I was more than his bridge partner. I was his friend. And now to hear this."

"It just goes to show you," said Sally McGonigle with a wistful sigh. "You never know. You just never, never know."

"Yeah, sure. Look, are you and your pals planning to hang around?" Kincannon asked Piper.

"The country, you mean?"

"That's exactly what I mean."

"Well, I can't speak for my teammates, of course, but personally, I could use a rest after all this excitement. I'm contemplating a cruise to the islands. St. Maarten might be nice. I hear there's an excellent keno game at the Concord Hotel."

"Wow, put me down for that," said McGonigle. "Sounds terrif!"

"Me too!" said Graves.

"Agent Haskins," Piper inquired, "have you ever played keno? Quite an intriguing game, from all accounts. I'm told that like chess, backgammon and bridge, it offers considerably more potential for... exploitation, shall we say, than at first meets the eye."

Not choosing to listen to any more of this banter, Inspector Kincannon rose to his feet and started forcing his way toward the aisle. "I'll want to see your report on this mess by Wednesday afternoon, Mr. Feinglass. Then, starting Thursday, you can take two or three weeks off. A month, if necessary."

"I don't need a vacation."

"Oh I'm not talking about a vacation exactly. Let's call it administrative leave. I get this feeling you've been pushing yourself too hard, Mr. Feinglass, much too hard. Not a good idea at your age, if you know what I mean. But we can talk about all of this on Wednesday." As he lumbered toward the back of the hall, he called over his shoulder, "My limo leaves for the airport in two minutes. Anybody who wants a lift better move it."

Long after he thought he was alone, Solomon Feinglass sat

195

motionless in the dark auditorium, staring at, but not focusing on, the screen. He did not wish to stay there, but found he was physically unable to leave; that he could not seem to stir himself from his seat. Just when he began to suspect that he had lost all feeling in his limbs, the weight of a hand on his shoulder gave him a start.

"We all had it wrong," said Deborah Croft. "Not just you. All of us."

"That's not exactly true," he replied with a wan smile. "Don't you remember back on the plane when Tulliver insisted there was nothing funny about that diary? I see now he was trying to warn us from the start."

Several minutes passed before either of them spoke again. "What are you going to do now?" Croft finally asked.

"I'll tell you, Deborah, I'm starting to see the wisdom in what the Inspector was saying. I believe the man has a point."

"You mean about your needing a rest?"

"That's right. A month of leave might be just the ticket. In fact, I've already begun thinking about where I might go."

"Really?"

"Yes, I'm contemplating a cruise to the islands..."

ABOUT THE AUTHOR

Novelist, playwright, biographer and composer Terry Quinn has had numerous short stories, poems and essays published in national magazines and literary journals. Seven of his plays have had Off-Broadway, regional, European or National Public Radio productions, including three music theater works for which he wrote the book, score and lyrics.

He has performed his own poetry and drama in New York City, London, Frankfurt and Paris, and played the lead role in the National Geographic film *It's About Time*, for which he wrote the screenplay.

The author lives in Brooklyn Heights, New York, where he teaches acting and creative writing.

For other fine titles from
VIVISPHERE PUBLISHING
visit
www.vivisphere.com

or call for a catalogue:
1-800-724-1100